The Descent of the Sons of God (A Parable)

BY

Marye Nicholas

This book is a work of non-fiction. Names and places have been changed to protect the privacy of all individuals. The events and situations are true.

© 2004 by Marye Nicholas. All rights reserved.

No part of this book may be reproduced, stored in a retrieval system, or transmitted by any means, electronic, mechanical, photocopying, recording, or otherwise, without written permission from the author.

ISBN: 1-4107-8363-4 (e-book)
ISBN: 1-4107-8364-2 (Paperback)

Library of Congress Control Number 2003097419

This book is printed on acid free paper.

Printed in the United States of America
Bloomington, IN

1stBooks - rev. 12/18/03

FRONT COVER

PAINTING: CELESTIAL DESCENT – ARTIST, JOEL ANTHONY

Joel Anthony, creator of "Illuminations of life," brings to life a world that exists, just beyond the boundaries of reality. Born in 1976 and raised in Tulsa, Oklahoma, Joel began his journey to be an artist at the age of three. As a child, he spent a fair amount of time not only in the city, but also in the fields and forests that surrounded his home. In these woods he would traverse many trails, logs and streams to discover the wonders that the forest held. As he walked the many trails he would have to stop and decide which path he wanted to take: there has always been something fascinating about the mystery of what lies beyond, that which you can't see. You can see and appreciate this, in the paintings of JOEL ANTHONY, as there is a mystery about the pieces: in fact the natural meets the supernatural. It is in these dreams and visions where the spiritual aspect of his work is manifested: he bridges the gap between the physical and the spiritual to bring into existence, "ILLUMINATIONS OF LIFE."

DEDICATION

I want to humbly thank all of my friends and family, who have prayed for me and encouraged me; becoming my cheering section as I completed each chapter of my book. I am also dedicating this book to the memory of my daddy; Rev R.A. Norman who stepped into the spirit realm in 1998. Also, Franklin Nicholas, who crossed over in 1995 has encouraged me many times in my dreams to complete what my heavenly father had put within me. Most of all I dedicate this book to my mother, Pauline Norman, and my son, Jonathan Nicholas.

Mother was a very talented writer as a teenager. Her greatest desire was to develop this gift as a writer of novels. She would mesmerize the children in her neighborhood with pages and pages of exciting tales and mystery stories. Her aspirations became secondary and eventually became latent, as over the years she would raise six children. Over the last two years mother has read each chapter as I finished them; keeping silent, yet, approving. Thank you mother for the gift you passed on to me.

Jonathan, my son; a minister, pastor and business executive; successful in each, I want to thank you for the many times you flew from Indiana to Tulsa, Oklahoma. During those visits we excitedly shared our thoughts and revelations of the word. You wowed me and awed me with your knowledge and I hope I affected you in the same way. What was important was the fact that we listened to each other.

Because there was so much information and revelation that the Lord was giving to me, I would burst forth like a fountain in words and tears; you listened. You were never negative, you were always positive; because you trusted my walk with my father, you knew I heard his voice. You are my seed and one day I will pass on to you the "double portion." Now son I'm not out of here yet! There is much more to come!

According as he has chosen us in him before the foundations of the world; that we should be holy and without blame before him in love. (Ephesians 1:4)

INTRODUCTION

I WANT TO EMPHASIZE that the first part of this book is a parable, allegory or story based on the scripture in Ephesians 1:4. We talk about the here and now, not realizing we have always been in him. Since there are no boundaries to the spirit, I can truthfully say, WE NEVER LEFT HIM. Jesus said in the New Testament, "No man has ascended Up to heaven, but he who has come down from heaven, even the son of man who is in heaven." (JOHN 3:13) The spirit of man is God and is with God at all times.

I want to stir your understanding of a father who loves his children far beyond the human's capacity to love. Believe me, God is emotional toward us! I have heard ministers, teachers and ministries say, "Because God was so lonely and he wanted a family, He created sons and daughters so that, He could pour out all of his love upon them." NO! A THOUSAND

TIMES NO! A NEW DAY WAS DAWNING! A NEW THING WAS BEING INTRODUCED! A NEW SPECIES, SONS OF GOD, TAKEN OUT OF HIMSELF AND PLACED INTO HUMAN BODIES! Talk about placement of sons, he took of his own spirit and placed it (Himself) into human bodies and put us on this earth, as Sons of God, to accomplish and fulfill his plan.

WHY WOULD GOD BE LONELY? We were already in him as a family, a spiritual family! My friend, if God were lonely, he would be incomplete. He is complete in himself for God is a self-sufficient God. He is all and all, and in all. Everywhere you look, all creation, planets, universes, galaxies and all space, beyond our ability to fathom intellectually or see, millions of light years away, are created by him. Ephesians 1:4 states, "According as he has set a course, completed in us a plan, selecting us in himself before the conception of the world, that we should be innocent, perfect, clean and pure, without fault, wrong, or disgrace; unblemished before him in love." All things began in father; our spirit is the substance of his spirit, the evidence of the many manifestations of himself. He continually divides and multiplies himself, yet he does not deplete the magnanimity of the enormity of his spirit.

Can you believe we were in him when he created the earth? We were experiencing first hand, his creative power, moving and having our complete being in him; functioning as a family. When you read this parable you will laugh, cry and worship. I believe you will understand the truth about our father that you have never experienced up to this present time. Children, we are sons, we are a family that made its way back to the father; back to his bosom where we originated. He waited for our return, to be placed back into him, to fulfill our destiny, as sons in the earth.

When were we placed back into him as sons? When Jesus rose from the dead and returned to the glory that he had before he came to the earth. "And the glory which you gave me, I have given to them; that they may be one as we are one." The glory Jesus gave us was his glory as a son. Jesus the PATTERN SON who was sent to bring us back to father reinstated us, so we could fulfill and finish the course and plan he had ordained. Before the foundations of the earth, Jesus was and always will be in the bosom of the father. We were and always will be in Christ, in the bosom of the father. We LIVED and now live in the very heart and emotions of God, AS A FAMILY and AS SONS. IN OTHER WORDS WE WERE and are THE VERY ESSENCE AND EXPRESSION OF HIS LOVE IN CHRIST, IN THE HEART OF FATHER. When I use the word US, I am talking about the spirit of man. It was the spirit of man that was returned to its glory that it had before the transgression.

As you read the parable and the teaching that follows you will find a similarity to the present days sons, functioning as a family, living and moving in the fullness of the spirit.

The Descent of the Sons of God (A Parable)

PART ONE: A PARABLE

Marye Nicholas

The Descent of the Sons of God (A Parable)

Suddenly Thousands Of Lights Appeared Everywhere, Bursting Forth Through The Night; A GALAXY WAS BORN!

Chapter 1

There was a father; he was an exceptional father and he had many sons. The sons were very close to their father; they lived and loved in unity. Everywhere the father went, the sons went also; when you saw the father you saw the sons. The sons walked like their father and talked like him, inheriting all of his characteristics and manners. You could not separate them or distinguish them from one another. It was awesome; they were the exact image of their father.

You could never quite identify who was talking when the father and sons were together. Peals of laughter would explode from their mouths as they feasted together, sharing their stories and exploits of valor. Their countenance would beam as they relived their great adventures in conversations that could mesmerize and fascinate the youngest of listeners.

Marye Nicholas

They were a family that loved one another wholeheartedly and a family connected together by one spirit.

While observing the father and sons, it was as if you were looking into many dimensions; looking closer you could see the father in the sons and the sons in the father. In a deeper sense, you could swear that you saw the sons stepping out of the father and the father stepping out of the sons.

The father was very creative; he would call to his sons very early each morning to come with him to new places and new universes. Every day was a NEW DAY full of wonder, curiosity and awe in the minds of the sons. Today their father would take them to the uttermost parts of the north; in this hemisphere there was a need for greater light. Father unfolded his plan for a new galaxy before them, and they agreed that the plan was excellent.

There was anticipation and excitement as their father raised his head and focused his attention, to the place of darkness in the heavens, creative words of wisdom came forth from his mouth. Tenderly he expressed emotions of love and concern as his presence hovered over the universe. Suddenly a twinkling as the twinkling of an eye was seen in the heavens. There was a commotion, as the swarming of Fireflies, in the distance. A birthing was taking place and starlight began to appear. Father's voice became as soft as the voice of a young mother while giving birth; assuring her unborn child that there was nothing to fear. He cooed and coaxed his creation as a loving doting father. Thousands of lights began to appear,

The Descent of the Sons of God (A Parable)

bursting forth through the night, A GALAXY WAS BORN!

The Sons of God clapping their hands rejoiced exclaiming, "the heavens declare the glory of God and the firmament shows his handiwork. Day unto day it utters speech, night unto night shows knowledge." Moving closer to their father they expressed their love in words of praise. They praised him for his magnificent creativity and vowed never to cease to be in awe of his wisdom and knowledge.

The beauty of the works of his hands was seen everywhere and the brilliance of their father transcended all intellect. Their father filled the earth and universes with his fullness of life. He was the fullness of all things.

The sons looked on marveling as their father stood surveying and observing the things he had created. All of a sudden he became so magnified, that the universe diminished at his presence. FATHER BECAME THE UNIVERSE! COULD THAT BE? NO, THE UNIVERSE BECAME THE FATHER! The galaxies, planets, sun, moon and all heavenly bodies were clothed in him. All things evolved and revolved in him.

In the magnitude of his glory, the Sons of God could see their father reach out and lovingly touch the finished products of his creation. He began explaining to and instructing them of their life, purpose, and ordination. Pleiades, Orion and Arcturus bowed to him and the constellation of the north, south, east and west brightened the heavens with blazing lights, as they recognized their God and Creator.

Marye Nicholas

For millions of years the Sons of God had seen him, who was the center of all things, do wonderful exploits with detailed preciseness. The summation of all of his workmanship was BEAUTY, LIGHT AND PERFECTION.

Knowing the thoughts of his sons, the father turned and spoke to them, "where were you my sons when I laid the foundations of the earth and the measures thereof and also the corner stone?" "We were in you father," the sons replied. Yes my sons you are, were and shall always be in me forever! You were in me when I laid the foundations of the earth and when I fastened it by my word, you heard the morning stars sing together and you my sons shouted for joy. So shall it be through endless time; you will always be in me rejoicing at the works of my hands. You are crowned with my glory and honor, you are my glory, my spirit, my works are your works and your works are my works. What you see me do, you do also; we are one. The Sons of God bowed their heads in agreement knowing their father was right. It was true; there was no love as great as their father's love for his children.

The Descent of the Sons of God (A Parable)

"I Have Created The Heavens And Formed The Earth, I Have Formed It To Be Inhabited."

Chapter 2

A NEW DAY of rest and recreation found the sons of God going forth throughout the heavens. Quietness prevailed over the atmosphere as father and his sons rode upon the wings of the wind. Accompanying them was an entourage of twenty thousand chariots and thousands of angels. The heavenly hosts rejoiced at his presence, and their voices went to the ends of the worlds as they exclaimed with praise, "Lift up you heads oh gates, even lift them up ye everlasting doors and the king of glory shall come in. Who is the king of glory? The lord of hosts, he is the king of glory!"

Within his magnificent glory, father's face radiated light as the brightness of the sun; he was a king over his kingdom. The heavenly hosts bowed at his presence and rejoiced as the heavens were filled with his glory. In the splendor of the moment, as the

Marye Nicholas

effulgence of light penetrated the very atmosphere, father, turned to his sons saying, "Come my sons we must go and command the morning and let the dayspring know its place. We will enter into the springs of the sea and in the search of the deep. We will find the way where light dwells and the direction the light parts to scatter the east wind upon the earth. My sons, we will set the ordinances of heaven, to have dominion and influence in the earth. I have created and formed the earth. I have formed it to be inhabited and have perceived the breadth of the earth; I laid the measures thereof and stretched the line upon it."

Father had made the earth and prepared it for habitation; the workmanship was phenomenal. As a sower he had gone forth to sow seed upon the earth and his words of wisdom were seeds sown, bringing forth life everywhere. He had separated the light from the darkness, after he had introduced light into a planet of great darkness. The light would be life to all the earth and would be life to all mankind. In wisdom he created all things for the pleasure of man, who would be placed upon the earth.

"COME SIT WITH ME MY SONS, I WANT TO TELL YOU A MYSTERY." The time had come for father to talk to his sons about his plans for their future. Lovingly he called each one to him, calling them by their name. HE KNEW, as he watched them, they would forever be engraved in his mind; they had been with him forever. They were his spirit and would eternally be his spirit. Although they were predestined to go forth into the earth, they would still be in him.

"My sons you have been with me from everlasting to everlasting; from the beginning or ever the

The Descent of the Sons of God (A Parable)

earth was. When there was no depth and fountains abounding with water. Before the mountains were settled, before the hills, you were in me. When the earth was not yet made, or the fields, or the highest part of the dust of the earth, you were in me. When I prepared the heavens, you were in me. When I established the clouds above and strengthened the fountains of the deep, when I gave to the sea my decree that the waters should not pass my commandments; when I appointed the foundations of the earth, you were with me. You were brought up with me, you were my daily delight rejoicing always before me; rejoicing that the earth would be inhabited with the sons of men. YOU MY SONS WILL BE THE SONS OF MEN!" "FATHER!" cried the Sons of God "What do you mean, we will be the sons of men!" "WE ARE THE SONS OF GOD, WE ARE YOUR SONS!" Father's voice was full of emotion as he gathered his children around him. "Come, it is tine to hear the mystery. I am going to tell you a plan that was ordained before the heavens and the earth were created. The mystery I am talking about, you will understand now; yet a day will come when the remembrance of it, will be wiped from your memory." Knowing this, father looked into the spirit realm far into the future, into a dimension that only he was aware of. Yes, yes, there it was; the plan was ordained and carried out. One day his sons would come to know again the many facets and expressions of love and wisdom of their father. It would take thousands of years to bring them to this place. There it was the END RESULT! They knew who they were, where they carne from and where they were going. They would realize they had never left him; they were always with him. ONCE AGAIN they would RETURN and feast together in him. FATHER REJOICED! THE SONS OF GOD WEPT.

The Descent of the Sons of God (A Parable)

The Father Of Lights And His Sons Were Standing On A Paved Work Of Sapphire Stone.

Chapter 3

Father's heart was full of compassion and love for his sons and they wept and talked among themselves. He knew they couldn't bear the thought of being separated from him. He must explain to them in comforting words while assuring them; although they would leave, they would never be separated from him. They would always be in him and one with him. The future, present life, death, powers or principalities or any other creature could not separate them from his love. His sons were the fullness of and the depth of his love; nothing or anyone could keep them from returning to him. Knowing nothing at this moment he could say would penetrate their sorrow, he spoke softly to them, "Tomorrow we will go into the earth and we will walk together and talk of your destiny. My sons you were blessed, chosen and pre-ordained to come forth from me before the foundations

Marye Nicholas

of the earth were ever laid. The stage is set; you will be as actors in a play, acting out your lives and experiences on earth in a human body experiencing humanity. Each of you will be a portion of me and have a portion of my spirit. Come now, and let's go, we will talk more. I know you do not understand now, but I will open your understanding as I explain."

A NEW DAY was dawning when the Sons of God came to present themselves before their father. Rays of light slowly spread across the sky, swallowing the darkness, as the sun took its place in the heavens. As darkness faded in the distance, the FATHER OF LIGHTS and his sons were standing on a paved work of sapphire stone; it was as blue as the sky, it looked as though it were the body of heaven in its clearness. As an artist unveils his prized painting, father unveiled the earth to his sons. It was a masterpiece of perfection. The Sons of God rejoiced declaring, "The earth is the Lord's and the fullness thereof, for you have laid the foundations of the earth and your right hand spanned the heavens. When you call unto them, they stand up together." Suddenly, the heavens and the earth were filled with praise. All the earth began to worship the Lord and sing unto him. The earth began to sing unto his name. The lands made a joyful noise and the trees clapped their hands. The hills skipped like lambs and the mountains like rams at the presence of the Lord, truth sprang out of the earth and righteousness and peace kissed each other. The Sons of God cried out in delight, "How excellent is your name in all of the earth oh Lord, you set your glory above the heavens." As their words went throughout the heavens and the earth, all creation bowed before their creator. The sun, moon,

The Descent of the Sons of God (A Parable)

stars, and the hosts joined in the praise and bowed before him. Their sound was the sound of music, as a great symphony with a choir of thousands of voices rising to a crescendo and then descending into a soft tone, becoming one voice. Father stood before the whole universe and earth with his hands raised as a beloved conductor; conducting his orchestra with the sounds of strings, winds, harps and voices. The sons stood reverently listening to the voices of music and praise fill the universe. They were aware that not only did the music and praise come from his creation it was also coming from their father. His face shined again as the brightness of the sun in its strength. His words of love and blessings went forth in a beautiful melody that ministered to all creation, individually and corporeally. Father stood in a place without time, lost in his love and adoration of his workmanship, rejoicing while dwelling in their praises.

    The sons of God walked with their father in the earth. The earth was a garden, a paradise full of trees, foliage and blossoms, shimmering and dancing in cascades of colors with each movement. Their father had opened the rivers in high places and fountains in the midst of valleys. The water in the sea, rivers and brooks flowed in harmony; their sound was as the sound of bubbling streams, running softly and gently over the rocks and pebbles. He planted in the wilderness the cedar, shittah, myrtle and the oil trees; and in the desert, fir, pine and the box trees. All of the trees in unison swayed with the wind, humming a song ever so softly. Animals moved quickly and quietly among the trees, with graceful leaps, jumping from rock to rock in the hills and mountains. The cattle and beasts of the field, the whole earth was created for the pleasure of man.

The moon, stars and the heavenly hosts, the works of father's hands, would be given to his sons to rule. Father would visit him, instruct and teach him. They would be the sons of God in the earth, made in his image, but clothed in flesh.

In the beginning man's soul was the personality of the spirit because, the spirit and soul were one; innocent and holy and righteous, crowned with the glory of the father. The soul would be the outer expression of the spirit, manifesting its fruitfulness and producing the evidence of that fruitfulness by the works of his hands. He would be guarded and protected by his spirit, which would be the spirit of his father in him, A TREE OF LIFE.

As they walked and talked together, father, as a loving shepherd, reached down and gathered two lambs in his arms and carried them in his bosom. Tenderly he stroked the young, as his eyes looked into their innocent and beautiful faces. Sadly he shook his head as if visualizing in his mind, something he didn't want to see. In a voice that was barely audible he said, "Behold the Lamb of God!" His sorrow turned to joy.

The time had come to talk to his sons of their destination. They ascended into a high mountain. In that high place he called his sons to him. "Come, my sons, come and sit with me." As they came before him again he called each one by their name, as they took their places beside him. Father felt as if his heart would burst from the love he felt for his many sons. They made him feel complete, and he was complete in them.

The Descent of the Sons of God (A Parable)

The beauty of the view from the highest place where they sat awed the sons of God. From the high place of the mountain one could see forever rolling terrains of hills carpeted with trees and shrubbery. Suddenly, their father's voice interrupted their thoughts. Softly he spoke to them, "I want to tell you a parable." The sons reverently gave him their attention with their eyes intently on his face he began. "There was a man who had two sons."

Marye Nicholas

The Descent of the Sons of God (A Parable)

When He Was A Great Distance From His Father's House, His Father, Whom Had Never Stopped Looking For His Son, Saw Him And Began To Run Down The Road Toward Him.

Chapter 4

The younger son said to his father, "Give to me the portion of my inheritance that you have willed to me." The father divided to them houses, servants, land, cattle and all of his wealth that he himself had accumulated during his lifetime. A few days passed and the younger son decided he would leave his father's house and make his home in a far away country. The time had come for his departure. He quickly gathered all his goods together to make his journey. There were numerous tears, goodbyes and embraces as the father sent him on his way with his blessings. As the father stood alone looking on, the son would turn constantly looking over his shoulder at his father waving to him in the distance.

In his travel across country, the younger son's thoughts were full of memories of his father and brother; the laughter, tears, and the closeness they shared as father, son and siblings. As these thoughts passed through his mind they stirred up warm feelings inside of him; giving him inner strength as the miles increased between him and home. There was an excitement in the air about him; this was a new adventure and he would make his father proud of him. He would become very wealthy and he would do it all by himself.

The father stood alone watching his son until he could no longer see him in the distance. He was very sorrowful and already he missed his son. In his mind he visualized him in the field feeding the animals and plowing with the oxen. He could hear his laughter and his footsteps. He could sense his son's presence everywhere. He turned to go into the house. He began talking to himself in a low tone as if his son was walking beside him, "I'm sending you forth my son into the world. I bless you to multiply in the earth, by taking that which is mine, investing and spending wisely and increasing your inheritance. One day at an appointed time you will return to me and will feast and rejoice with me in my house again."

The younger son settled in a far country. As time went by he forgot his goals and the promises he made to himself and to his father. He took pride in having many friends and he liked having them all around him. He was very attentive to their counsel and advice. Their voices were constantly in his ear, coaxing and pressuring him to invest in worthless projects and money markets. Their words held no wisdom, nor had any substance, and as the years went by he failed to take advantage of good opportunities. His inheritance, which

The Descent of the Sons of God (A Parable)

had consisted of money, servants, cattle, and land, the very essence of his father's livelihood, was being depleted.

In his personal life the younger son indulged, without restraint, in wild loose living. His extreme appetite for sensual pleasures was leading him morally astray and leaving him corrupt and depraved. When he was with his friends he was loud and boastful, engaging in and inciting public disturbances. At this point of his life he was out of control and he could not help himself.

The younger son had spent all of his money and all that his father had so graciously given him. All of his friends had forsaken him; his friendship had no monetary value to them anymore. They left him devastated and set out to find their next victim of prey.

Realizing what his life had been reduced to, and knowing what he had foolishly done, he knew he had to work for someone, or he would die. The younger son hired himself out for labor to a citizen of that country because the son had nothing and a famine ravaged the land where the son lived.

The youngest was sent into the field to feed swine. Day after day, while he was weak from hunger, he would watch the swine as he fed them. He craved the husks of the swine, and in the deliria caused from a lack of food, he imagined himself filling his belly with their food. In a state of starvation, no one gave to him or helped him. He was despairing of life and was brought down to the dust of earth.

As he lay there he came to himself and said aloud, "How many of my father's servants have bread in their houses to eat, and excess to share with others?

Marye Nicholas

I will get up and go to my father's house and say to my father, I have been wrong, I have rebelled against you, I didn't keep your counseling, teaching and advice while I was away from you. I was prideful and arrogant, sinning against you. Father, please hire me as one of your servants for I am not worthy to be your son." As he rose to his feet he rehearsed these words of contrition over and over, leaving behind all the filth that oppressed him. Then he began his journey back home to his father.

When the younger son was a great distance from his father's house, his father whom never stopped looking for his son saw him. Covering the distance between them, he ran down the road with his heart pounding, his eyes filled with tears as he drew closer. He was amazed at his son's emaciated appearance. His amazement turned to pity and compassion as he embraced his child. He wept over and over as he held his face in his hands and kissed him. Words of sorrowful repentance poured from the young son's lips, as he held his father tightly in an embrace that was evident of his submission. He exclaimed loudly, "Father I have sinned against you and heaven; I am no longer deserving to be your child!" Before he could open his mouth to ask his father if he could be his servant, the father called his servants to him and said, "Go quickly! Bring the best robe and put it on my son. Bring a ring for his hand and shoes for his feet." He also instructed his servants to kill the fatted calf and invite all of his friends to celebrate his son's return. "Let everyone dance, sing, rejoice and be merry; my son, who was dead, is now alive again. He was lost and now he is found."

The Descent of the Sons of God (A Parable)

The elder son was very angry and refused to join the celebration. The father hearing of this talked with his elder son entreating him to enter into festivities. The son refused answering, "Many years I have served you, and I have not at anytime transgressed your commandments. Father, you have never given me a kid that I might be merry with my friends. As soon as your younger son, which devoured your living with harlots, came home; you began celebrating his return and have killed the fatted calf for him." The father looked tenderly at his older son and spoke with compassion, "Son you are still with me, all that I have is yours. It is appropriate to celebrate and be glad. Your brother was dead and is alive again. He was lost and now he is found."

Marye Nicholas

The Descent of the Sons of God (A Parable)

They Ascended Into The Heavens Above The Earth, Riding Upon A Cloud, To Sit Upon The Circle Of The Earth.

Chapter 5

It was twilight when father finished the parable. The sons of God were very quiet as they reflected on their father's words. Father knew that there were many questions his sons wanted to ask, for he knew the ways of his sons so well. He loved them as his own body; they were his body. When they were ready and wanted to talk, they would come to him.

As night descended, the sons watched their father as he stood to his feet and walked slowly down the mountain. They marveled when suddenly his very presence became a great light that penetrated the blanket of darkness around them. The glory of that light went before him. The moon's light was magnified, casting a silvery glow over the earth, touching and caressing all creation. The stars in the universe were as glittering jewels of light illuminating the heavens. Although he had made the sun to rule by day and the moon by night, father was the light of the world. He covered himself with light as with a garment. He was clothed with honor and majesty. His brightness was as the light and he had light coming out of his hands; for his hands were the hiding of his power.

The Sons of God talked among themselves as they hurriedly followed in their father's glorious light and footsteps. Looking into the heavens they exalted him, declaring with praise, "Let the moon praise you and the stars of light, the heavens of heavens are yours, they praise your wonders. Who in heaven can be compared unto you father, who among the sons of the mighty can be likened unto you?" Father turned slowly toward his sons as he listened to their words of adoration and praise. Lovingly he replies, "You are lights in the world, you are like me! You are my image, look at yourselves!" It was true, they too were clothed in light, and the glory of their light brightened the world. They were like their father, THEY WERE SONS OF LIGHT.

In the descent down the mountain the Sons of God began to talk among themselves of the parable their father had told them. They were so engrossed in their discussion they had not noticed that their father had slowed his pace with the intent to listen to their conversation. He knew they wanted to ask him questions and he was ready to explain the parable to them so they could understand. Father stopped, turned and looked into the eyes of his sons with a long searching gaze. He studied each face. Their countenance was open and innocent as they stood before him in his righteousness and holiness. Their thoughts were thoughts of concern for their future and their destiny.

The Descent of the Sons of God (A Parable)

Father gathered his sons into himself. They would go to a quiet place to talk, he knew the perfect place. They ascended into the heavens above the earth, RIDING UPON A CLOUD, TO SIT UPON THE CIRCLE OF THE EARTH. Suddenly, father's voice thundered through the heavens, "Lift up your eyes on high my sons and behold I have created these things. I bring out the host by number and I call them by their names. By the greatness of my might, because I am great in power, not one fails. I have measured the waters in the hollow of my hand and meted out the heaven with the span; comprehending the dust of the earth in a measure and weighed the mountains in scales and the hill in a balance. I am the everlasting God, the Lord, the creator of the ends of the earth. I faint not neither am I weary; I have spoken. You have asked me concerning things to come, concerning the works of my hands. It is for you to know the mystery of the parable. Listen carefully and I will begin the interpretation." The sons of God turned toward their father. The anticipation of the revelation they were about to hear was expressed on their faces. The brightness from their countenance became an aura of rainbow colors encircling their heads as halos. The sons of God looked like angelic beings and cherubs with innocent baby faces as they sat before their father waiting for his words.

Marye Nicholas

The Descent of the Sons of God (A Parable)

A Love That Could Never Be Measured Poured Forth From Their Very Being And Permeated The Air As A Beautiful Fragrance.

Chapter 6

Choosing his words very carefully, father began the explanation of his story. "My sons I am the certain man and you are the sons. Everything I have is yours. Each one of you is a part and portion of me. All of you will go into the earth at an appointed time and this will be your far away journey. All that I am will be within you; this is your inheritance and goods. I will divide all of my wealth and authority among you and the earth will be your possession. You are the lights of the world, the light bearers, the greater light that divides the darkness."

The sons of God nodded their heads in agreement and understanding as he continued. The soft tone of their father's voice seemed to draw them into the explanation until they could actually see themselves as characters acting out each word of a script. They were fascinated and intrigued as they listened to their father interpret the mystery to them. Father continued, "You have walked, talked and laughed with me from the beginning. I have taught you and you have seen my very life and existence. You have dwelled in my house forever, but you must take your inheritance and go into the earth to give my life, I have invested in you, to all mankind. You will be leaving my house, this dwelling place, and with my blessing, taking your goods to multiply and increase. As a corporate son you will encounter many voices of adverse counsel and advice. Eventually you will forget my words, laws and principles. You will choose at your own will to turn from me. You will fill your belly with unproductive and negative fruit, which will cause your life to waste away. Over a period of many years you shall come to hopelessness and depravity. You shall be brought down to the dust of the earth.

The sons of God were stunned at their father's words. It was more than they could

comprehend. Disobedience? Never! Rebellion? Never! How could this take place? They loved their father! Shaken and totally confused they cried out, "Father we could never rebel against you, you have been our dwelling place forever! You are our portion and inheritance; we are your portion and inheritance. Where would we go from your spirit? We are your spirit! We never want to flee from your presence. When we ascend into the heavens, you are there; then, we take the wings of the morning and dwell in the uttermost parts of the sea. You are there also and your hand upholds us and leads us. We are blessed to dwell in your house and will always be praising you."

The Descent of the Sons of God (A Parable)

Tears of sorrow flooded their eyes streaming down their innocent upturned faces. Their voices became inaudible overcome by their sobs of despair. A love that could never be measured poured forth from their very being and permeated the air as a beautiful fragrance. Father was gripped with compassion by their display of emotions. He quickly gathered his sons in his arms and held them tightly. Comforting them until their weeping subsided. Yet, he couldn't let their intense love and sorrow prevent his plan for their destiny; it was for their good.

For thousands of years the sons of God would be proven and tested. The finale would consummate in their return. They would return to the glory they had now in him. Only there would be a difference, they would be FULL GROWN SONS OF GOD sent into the earth, worlds, and new universes to teach, lead, govern and heal the nations.

Marye Nicholas

The Descent of the Sons of God (A Parable)

Your Feet Shall Be Shod With The Finest Of Shoes, So That You Can Walk In My Ways, And My Will, As King's Sons.

Chapter 7

In deep thought father searched the faces of each one of his sons. His explanation of the parable had troubled them, knowing this, he knew at this time he must sustain them. He had to restore their minds to peacefulness. With a thought from his mind, instantly, the sons of God found themselves with their father in a valley of plush green meadows and pastures that were clothed with flocks of sheep. The sons lay beside the still waters on the thick grass of the meadows, listening to the sound of the rippling waters of the brooks. What peacefulness they felt in this place. Father walked among his sons laying his hands upon their heads. The sons began to rejoice, "Surely goodness and mercy shall follow us all the days of our life and we shall dwell in your house forever. Father, you are our friend and companion. You are our shepherd, we shall not want."

Marye Nicholas

Father continued to comfort his sons with words of assurance as they reclined upon the grass. At that moment he decided to explain more of the parable. He expounded to them the importance to listen carefully to what he had to say. Submissive as sons, they gave him their full attention.

"There will come a day, my sons, when you will realize that you have spent your days in darkness and have filled your life with fruitless works of vanity. In hopelessness you will raise your voice in despair. As in the parable, the fatted calf shall be offered as a sacrifice for your sins. At that moment I will be waiting and listening, no matter how far you have fallen, I will lift you up. I will receive you back unto myself." When their father spoke of the fatted calf being sacrificed, the sons of God raised their heads looking directly into their father's eyes. He knew what they were thinking, for the expressions on their faces were as spoken words. "When you return to my house there shall be rejoicing, dancing and singing. I will give you glory and honor; glory and honor shall be as a robe of righteousness about you. I will give you authority and rulership as a ring encircling your finger; the evidence and seal of your of your sonship. Your feet will be shod with the finest of shoes, so that you can walk in my ways, and my will, as king's sons.

It was evening and the sun was setting. Splashes of colors in brilliant oranges and reds spilled over into the earth, giving the appearance of a painter's canvass, as he added to his painting the picturesque valley and meadows. The sheep ceased their grazing in the pastures as evening descended. The ewes lovingly

The Descent of the Sons of God (A Parable)

nudged their young as they followed closely beside their mothers to a place of rest.

Without a word, father led his sons through the valley of green meadows. They walked through fields of flowers that looked of iridescent colors from the lingering rays of the sun. The sons touched the velvety petals, breathing in the fragrance that penetrated the air as it hovered over the valley. Their eyes drank in all the beauty; they wanted to stay in this valley of peace and restoration forever.

The sons of God followed their beloved father through the fields wanting to be closer to him. The parable he had told them was more than they could comprehend. Suddenly father stopped, he held out his arms and gathered them into himself. No one spoke a word, there was nothing to say, there were no words to express their love for their father, nor words to express the father's love for his sons. They were in him and that was all that mattered.

Marye Nicholas

The Descent of the Sons of God (A Parable)

Their appearance had one likeness as if it were, a wheel in the middle of a wheel.

Chapter 8

Father stood overlooking and carefully observing the universe with his sons. THE SUN, MOON, STARS, PLANETS AND GALAXIES were functioning properly, and in order, at his word. Father began to explain to his sons the ordination, positions and influences of the solar system on the earth; pointing out to them that some of the stars were larger in size and brighter than the sun, yet the sun would keep other objects in orbit with its immense gravitational field. The whole truth was that father upheld all things by the word of his power. He stretched out the north over an empty place, and hangs the earth upon nothing. The sons of God were beginning to understand the importance of the power and authority of their father's word. He had endowed them with that same power, as sons, and crowned them with the glory of his spirit.

Marye Nicholas

A new day had burst forth with all of its hues of colorful splendor. The sun, rising slowly overhead, sent life giving light to the earth. Every plant of the field, every herb, every tree, every fruitful tree and every blade of grass responded to its light; raising their heads as children with dew on their brow, lifting their faces to be kissed by the morning sun. It was a day of rejoicing; a moment in time and eternity appointed to all creation to become one voice in praise. The heavenly bodies, the earth, the heavenly hosts, angels, archangels, cherubim and seraphim gathered together before their creator to exalt and magnify him for his wondrous workmanship. It was time for father's plan to be carried out. The finishing touches would be the placement and descent of the sons of God into the earth. However, yet to be revealed was the salvation of man, the Messiah and the fatted calf.

The sound of voices filled the air as the singing and rejoicing began. The sons of God were leaping, dancing and praising God. The heavenly host of angels joined in saying, "Praise ye the Lord, for it is good to sing praises unto our God. Praise him all ye hosts, praise him all ye heavens of heavens and ye waters above the heavens, for you commanded and they were created. You established them forever. Praise him in his sanctuary and in the firmament of his power. Let us dance and sing praises unto his name." The sons of God took hold of each other's hands, making a circle around their father, increasing their speed as they danced. The angels formed another circle dancing and singing as one voice. The third circle consisted of the cherubim and seraphim singing and praising as they all danced around their heavenly creator. ALL SPIRIT

The Descent of the Sons of God (A Parable)

BEINGS WERE CHILDREN OF LIGHT, AND AS EACH GROUP REVOLVED AROUND THEIR FATHER, THEIR APPEARANCE HAD ONE LIKENESS, AS IF IT WERE, A WHEEL IN THE MIDST OF A WHEEL.

The celebration ceased and a reverence moved over the atmosphere. The many voices praising silently, became a humming sound, echoing through the heavens. There was an atmosphere of expectancy that was electrifying. Sadness, sorrow, and compassion crossed the face of their father as he stepped forward. When the humming became voluminous, father lifted his hand into the air motioning like one pulling back a veil. The humming ceased, it was as if all creation gasped to catch their breath. Caught by surprise, the sons of God spoke out in unison, "The fatted calf!" Father cried out with a loud voice, "BEHOLD THE LAMB OF GOD!"

THERE BEFORE THEM WAS A BRAZEN ALTER, and bound to the horns of the alter was a lamb that was slain. SUDDENLY, out of the brazen alter appeared two wooden beams made into a cross. The sons of God were speechless, WAS THIS THEIR FATHER HANGING ON A CROSS? NO, IT WAS ONE LIKE THEM! COULD IT BE? IT HAD TO BE! YES, IT WAS A SON OF GOD! He was bound to the cross, as the lamb was tied to the horns of the alter. HE WAS LIFTED UP AND SUSPENDED BETWEEN HEAVEN AND EARTH.

Marye Nicholas

The Descent of the Sons of God (A Parable)

Deliver your darling, your only one, your only son from death.

Chapter 9

There was silence in the heavens and in the spirit realm. In the earth, not one creature stirred or made a sound; not even the trembling of a leaf could be seen. TIME HAD STOPPED AS ALL CREATION LOOKED UPON THE LAMB OF GOD. His face was cut, bruised and swollen. His beard was pulled from his face, forcing the blood to surface, and causing the skin to hemorrhage. A plaiting of thorns that circled his head resembling a crown, pressed deeply into his forehead. The blood from the thorns oozed slowly from his brow onto his face and shoulders. There were open lacerations on his chest and back, while blood and water continued to flow from the wound in his side. In addition to his intense suffering, his hands and feet were nailed to the cross. His pain was excruciating. He was without form and void; and darkness was upon the face of the deep. Darkness, destruction, ruin and death were upon him.

He was an abomination to the desolate. He was wasted and empty, worthless humanity.

The sons of God wept as they looked intently, with compassion, on the face of the Lamb of God; while asking one another, "Is this the fatted calf father was talking about in the parable? Who is he?" Their minds were full of questions. It was imperative for them to talk to their father. In the midst of their words and thoughts, a voice in agony and unbearable pain came from the cross. The sons raised their heads to listen to his words. What was it about this one that was so familiar? They moved closer to the cross, standing beneath it. Their eyes were fixed on him.

THE LAMB OF GOD CRIED OUT, "Father, my father, why have you deserted me? You have not reached out your hand to help me. I have cried to you constantly day and night but you do not hear me. As an infant I was cast upon you. You gave me hope and sustained me while my mother nurtured me. Don't leave me for trouble is near, there is no one to protect me. I am poured out like water as a drink offering. My bones are stretched and are out of joint. My soul is terrified; fear makes my bowels melt like wax, taking away my strength. My mouth is dry and my tongue sticks to my jaws. You have brought me to the dust of the earth. I am a worm, no man, brought face to face with death. The wicked surround me and close in on me, piercing my hands and my feet. Father, my father, my strength, please hasten to help me. Deliver my soul from the blow of your hand. Deliver me from the pain that is like a sharp knife cutting away my life. Save me from the devouring mouth and teeth of the enemy. Hear me as the sacrificial lamb. Hear me from the horns of the altar.

The Descent of the Sons of God (A Parable)

DELIVER YOUR DARLING, YOUR ONLY ONE, YOUR ONLY SON FROM DEATH."

"Deliver your darling your only one, your only son," repeated the sons of God. "We are your sons! Father, explain these word to us," they exclaimed. Father looked at his sons sadly, saying, "Look at me." The sons of God looked into their father's eyes. Through his eyes love was expressed in depth without end. They were drawn into the depth of that love until they were one mind. Entering into his very being they saw time before the heavens and earth were created. What they saw in the spirit was the ordination and predestination of the LAMB OF GOD, THE SON OF GOD before the foundations of the earth were laid. Now they understood the parable! This was the sacrifice!

SUDDENLY the scene changed. The cross that stood before them was empty. Darkness was around them, and in that darkness a form of a man laid in the earth. As their eyes became accustomed to the blackness, they saw the form was wrapped with strips of linen and a cloth was placed over the face. Without a word, father stepped from out of the midst of the sons of God and entered into the depth of the earth. The light of his presence swallowed up the darkness, as life would swallow up death. Father stood before the form in the earth and began to speak. "You are the brightness of my glory and the exact image of my being. You have kept your word, fulfilling the law and purging the sins of the sons of men. You are my son and I am your father. This day, for this purpose, have I begotten you and forever shall your kingdom be established. You are anointed with the oil of gladness above your brethren, and your scepter is the scepter of righteousness. You will rule over the heavens, the earth and all creation. For all things are the works of your hands. The children were created flesh and blood, you took upon yourself the same; that through death you would destroy him that had the power of death. You were made like your brethren, that you might be a faithful high priest in things pertaining to God, to make reconciliation for the sins of the people; who through the fear of death were all their lifetime subject to bondage."

Suddenly the earth shook and trembled. The foundations of the hills moved and were shaken. There went up a smoke out of his nostrils, and a fire out of his mouth devoured. The voice of the HIGHEST, THUNDERED IN THE HEAVENS, "IT IS FINISHED!" A sound as a mighty wind filled the earth where father and his sons were standing. A surge of power from his hands entered into THE LAMB OF GOD, THE FIRST BEGOTTEN SON; lifting him out of his linen wrappings, yet, the encasement of strips remained intact, from the one hundred pounds of spices and ointment that his body was wrapped and bound in. As the Lamb of God stood to his feet, the father and the sons began to rejoice.

THE FIRST BEGOTTEN FROM THE DEAD was radiant. The light of the world, the Lamb of God, embraced his father and brethren fervently. Lifting his voice in praise, declaring to his father, "This shall be written of you to all generations to come. The people that shall be filled with your spirit shall praise. You have looked down from your sanctuary in heaven and beheld the earth; to hear the groaning of the prisoners

The Descent of the Sons of God (A Parable)

and to loose those that were appointed to death. I will declare your name unto my brethren and I will praise you. A seed shall serve you and a people shall be born that will declare your righteousness, and also declare that your father has done this.

When the FIRST BEGOTTEN SON finished his declaration of praise and exaltation to his father, he reached down and picked up the linen cloth. Folding it neatly, he laid it aside, separately, from the wrappings. Softly he repeated the words of his father, "You have laid the foundations of the earth, and the heavens are the work of your hands. They shall wax old and perish, but you shall endure. They shall wax old as a garment. As a garment you shall change them and fold them up." He knew the encasement of the wrappings and tomb was significant of death. He had put off death as a garment, folding it up and laying it aside to remain in the earth, to exist no longer. He put on a new garment of light, life and righteousness. The old age had ended and a new age had begun. When he had finished, he embraced his many member family; stepping into the bosom of his father, followed by the sons of God, ascending into the heavens.

Marye Nicholas

The Descent of the Sons of God (A Parable)

The Chasm Would Become The Womb For The Birthing Of The Earth.

Chapter 10

The Sons of God tried to piece together what they had seen of their father's plan and purpose for the future of man. Several things took precedence in their thoughts and conversations. One, they couldn't comprehend that they would become the "sons of men." Two, they agreed as they talked that the revealing of the LAMB OF GOD had been the most overwhelming revelation. Yet, there was more to be explained to them. They would be patient. The sons had learned many valuable lessons in such a short time; now they eagerly awaited the appearance of their father. Meanwhile as they waited for their father, they reflected on their many years of sonship. Their father was their past, present and future. He was their whole existence, their sanctuary and their dwelling place. They were a family, a city set in a higher dimension than that of the earth.

Marye Nicholas

The sons of God were laughing and talking to one another as they recalled the wonderful works father had made, created and fashioned by his hand. The faces of the sons brightened at the thought of the time he announced to them he would create a new world. This world would have its own universe, plants, galaxies, sun, moon and stars. Being in a state of excitement their father revealed to them his plan. He couldn't help but see the look of surprise on their faces. Undaunted by their gaze, he coaxed them with comforting words as he took them to a vast empty place in space. Although it was a vast empty abyss, his presence filled the length, depth and width of the great chasm. He took of his spirit and placed it in the abyss, whereas the chasm would become the womb for the birthing of the earth. As a great winged creature he hovered over the abyss, as creative words began to flow from his mouth; pouring forth as living waters into the abyss, becoming as a gushing of many waters. In a moment of time the depth of the chasm was filled and a huge body of water was suspended in time and space. Father stepped back, observing intently the evidence of his words. He saw it was good and continued. He moved back and forth over the waters, pacing and retracing his steps. He opened his arms wide and spread his hands toward the water, and with a thunderous voice, spoke substance into existence. Turning momentarily he gazed into the surrounding darkness, when suddenly a bubbling gurgling sound was heard from the depth of the chasm. The sound was the sound of an infant's muffled cry. Then father spoke, and the breath of his mouth became a wind that parted the channels of water. Out of the depth of the

The Descent of the Sons of God (A Parable)

chasm burst forth a gigantic sphere of substance, rising slowly, coming to rest above the waters. THE EARTH WAS BORN!

Father's face beamed with pride as his eyes went to and fro over the substance, examining his newborn, the first fruits of his creation. He doted over and cooed words of love as he molded and shaped the earth as a master potter. Gently he embraced the earth as a father embraces his firstborn. He clothed the earth in a garment of light and his word became a swaddling band to preserve, guard and protect, while holding it in its place.

He shut up the waters with bars and doors decreeing, "This is your place, and you will come no further!" He laid the measures and stretched the line upon it. By the word of his power he fastened the foundations of the earth in space and laid the cornerstone. He moved over the face of the deep and stepped quickly into the core of the earth. The light of his presence infiltrated the springs of the seas as he searched its depths. In the places of the deep where he walked, darkness dissipated; light and life took up residence. His spirit moved upon the surface of the earth sowing eternal life, saturating every inch of the soil, and preparing it for seed.

One thing remained for him to do before he sowed the seed of his word into the ground. He would create a higher realm, another dimension in the earth's atmosphere. He would build a city and lay the chambers of his house in the midst of it. HE WOULD CALL IT EDEN! THERE HE WOULD LIVE WITH HIS CHILDREN. East in Eden he would plant a garden and call it: "THE GARDEN OF GOD." A river would flow from Eden into the garden. From the garden it would separate, stretching abroad to the north, south, east and west; dividing into four bodies of water, lying foursquare in the highest places in the four corners of the earth. With a finishing touch, father balanced the clouds with his perfect knowledge and spread out the sky as a molten looking glass. Whatever the Lord pleased, that did he in heaven and in the earth, in the sea and all deep places.

The Descent of the Sons of God (A Parable)

The Throne Was Like A Fiery Flame.

Chapter 11

Father had allowed his sons to see the mystery of the FIRST BEGOTTEN SON, THE LAMB OF GOD BEFORE THE FOUNDATIONS OF THE EARTH WERE LAID. NOW HE WOULD ALLOW THEM TO SEE A NEW AGE THAT WOULD DAWN IN THE SPIRIT REALM. A new day of the resurrection power of the KING OF KINGS AND LORD OF LORDS.

It was a time of rejoicing. The harp, psaltery, organ and stringed instruments played a melody of praise, creating an environment of worship in the heavenly sanctuary. The angelic chorus lifted their voices in resonant exaltation singing, "Praise the Lord, praise God in his sanctuary, praise him in the firmament of his power. Praise him with the sound of a trumpet; praise him with a sound of a harp, timbrel and dance. Let everything that has breath praise the lord, praise ye the Lord." Thousands upon thousands of voices blended together in harmony, joining the chorus. Caught up in the moment of awe, ecstasy and praise, the sons of God heard behind them a great voice as a sound of a trumpet saying, "I AM ALPHA AND OMEGA THE FIRST AND THE LAST!" THEY TURNED TO SEE WHO WAS SPEAKING AND SAW SEVEN GOLDEN CANDLESTICKS. IN THE MIDST OF THE CANDLESTICKS, ONE LIKE UNTO THE SON OF GOD, THE LAMB OF GOD: THE FIRST BEGOTTEN FROM THE DEAD. He was clothed with a garment down to his feet and a golden girdle was around his waist. The hair of his head was white like wool, as white as snow. His eyes were very distinct and expressive and their look was as flames of fire. His feet were the color of brass, when they are burned in a furnace. When he spoke, his voice was the sound like the noise of many waters. Out of his mouth went the word of God, sharp as a two-edged sword and his countenance was as the sun in its strength. Every eye in the spirit realm beheld his glory and majesty as father's voice echoed through the heavens, in a reverberating sound, "You are a high priest forever, after the order of Melchizedec."

SUDDENLY THE SONS OF GOD WERE BEFORE THEIR FATHER'S THRONE. THE THRONE WAS LIKE A FIERY FLAME AND HIS FEET WERE AS A BURNING FIRE. Before the throne was a sea of glass like unto crystal and out of the throne room proceeded lightening, thundering and voices. A fiery stream issued and came forth from before him. Thousands upon thousands ministered unto him. Thousands times thousands stood before him. The Son of God, the first begotten from the dead, the Lamb of God was brought before the ANCIENT OF DAYS,

The Descent of the Sons of God (A Parable)

THEIR INFINITE FATHER. The ANCIENT OF DAYS gave him a NAME ABOVE EVERY NAME, A NAME IN HIS EXALTATION, NOT THE NAME OF HIS HUMANITY. THIS NAME WOULD NOT LIMIT HIM AS A SON, BUT GIVE HIM THE STATUS OF GOD HIMSELF. EVERY KNEE WOULD BOW AT THAT NAME AND EVERY TONGUE WOULD CONFESS THAT NAME IN HEAVEN AND IN EARTH, GIVING GLORY TO FATHER, FOR HE WAS GOD, HE WAS FATHER. HE WAS GIVEN A KINGDOM, DOMINION AND GLORY. ALL PEOPLE NATIONS AND LANGUAGES WOULD SERVE AND WORSHIP HIM. THIS DOMINION IS AN EVERLASTING DOMINION THAT SHALL NEVER PASS AWAY, OR BE DESTROYED.

As the sons of God stood before the throne, the Lamb of God looked lovingly upon them. His eyes pierced into the very depth of their being. The sons of God fell on their faces worshiping. He gathered them into his arms and wept loudly as the brightness of his love and glory filled the throne room. Just as if a conductor waved his wand so that the music would start on cue; all of heaven burst forth in a song as they danced and sang before him, "You are fairer than the children of men, grace is poured into your lips, your name is as an ointment poured forth, therefore God has blessed you forever. Father has set a crown of pure gold upon your head and clothed you with robes of royalty and righteousness!"

Marye Nicholas

The Descent of the Sons of God (A Parable)

The Procession Preceded Upward From Every Part Of The City And Their Appearance Was As Flames Of Fire.

Chapter 12

The CITY OF GOD was a joyous city. The holy city, the kingdom of righteousness, was built on a high mountain. "THE MOUNTAIN OF GOD." The measurements of the city were astounding to the eye of the beholder. In accessing its magnitude, in the dimension of the spirit, it covered the earth and seas. Only those who walked and lived in the realm of the spirit could see it.

In the city father had established and maintained an environment of worship and praise, a sanctuary, a habitation of quietness and peace. Daily in the temple melodious voices were raised in songs of praise to the soft notes of skilled players on stringed instruments and harps. In the streets laughter could be heard with the sound of feet dancing to the rhythm of pipes and tabrets. The music, dancing and laughter made glad the hearts of the hearers, as each son and angelic being went about the city to their assigned posts and duties.

In working and completing an assignment, the minds of the sons were always aware of their father's presence. Whatever they set their hand to do was with the intent to glorify him. It had nothing to do with acts of servitude, or the forcing of one's will. It was the love for their father that motivated their response to their responsibilities.

The strong city was established on twelve foundations of precious stones of jasper, sapphire, chalcedony, emerald, sardonyx, sardius, chrysolyte, beryl, topaz, chrysoprasus, jacinth and amethyst. The walls of the city were made of jasper, the whole city and the street of the city was made of pure gold. Polished gold that had the look of transparent glass. There were twelve entrances into the Holy City, at each entrance a gate made of one pearl.

In the realm of the spirit there was no darkness and there was no need for the light of the sun, moon, or stars. Father's presence and glory was the light of the city and the source of all light. Everything outside of the spirit realm received its light from created substance that came from him, the creator.

As the Sons of God went through the city with their father, he explained the purpose, and the plan of the city fully to them. He also mentioned that the city would be in continual preparation until an appointed time, smiling he added, "I have named the walls of this city SALVATION and the gates I will call PRAISE." While walking together upon the foundations of jewels, the light of father's presence illuminated the stones to such brilliant colors, that they looked as if

The Descent of the Sons of God (A Parable)

they were walking among stones of fire. To the observer outside of the HOLY CITY, the city from a distance looked as if it were a glowing shining ember. As they continued their walk, father would stop momentarily and slowly move his hand over the walls of jasper saying, "My sons, you are my precious stones. My jewels firmly established in the foundations of this city." The sons of God pondered over the words of their father. In their minds they envisioned the precious stones of the walls and foundations as a covering or cloak to those within the HOLY CITY.

The Temple was comprised of many chambers or rooms that their father had prepared for his sons. Massive pillars of support were placed in various areas of the structure. The sons had worshiped here as long as they could remember.

From the Temple mount came the sound of a trumpet, a signal to assemble and a call to worship. The voices of many thousands of angels echoed through the city "Come let us go up unto the mountain of the Lord, into the house of our God. Come with singing and enter his gates with thanksgiving, come enter his courts with praise." As the Sons of God and angelic beings ascended the Temple mount, they were clothed with splendor and glory. The procession proceeded upward, from every part of the city, and their appearance was as flames of fire. In their ascent into the Temple, every voice was lifted in praise. "Great is our Lord and greatly to be praised, glory an honor are in his presence, gladness and strength are in his place, come before him and worship him in the beauty of holiness. Our God reigns, our God reigns!"

Marye Nicholas

The Temple choir sang continually with the accompaniment of cymbals, harps and stringed instruments, as the director of the choir declared with a loud voice, "Stand up and worship the Lord your God!" The trumpets began to sound and the sons began to praise. The trumpets sounded and the sons praised. In their praising, the many voices became as one, as they lifted their hands saying, "GREAT IS OUR LORD! GREAT IS OUR LORD!"

Suddenly father stood in the midst of his sons; he was high and lifted up and his glory filled the Temple. The sons of God, angels, archangels and seraphim bowed on their knees crying, "HOLY, HOLY, HOLY!" As they praised and worshiped, out of the bosom of the father stepped the Lamb of God, the first begotten Son of God. He was dressed in a garment down to his feet, and a golden girdle about his waist. At his appearance, the light of the Temple was magnified a hundred fold, causing the pure gold of the Temple to reflect as mirrors in the sanctuary. The Sons of God looked with amazement into the glory. They saw their faces reflected in the Temple, chambers, walls, pillars, street and foundations. They were the reflection of that glory and the reflection of the Father and Son. At last they understood, all of the sons made up the Temple and the City. The sons of God *were* the HOLY CITY OF GOD!

The Descent of the Sons of God (A Parable)

Father Would Let Them Experience The Results Of Creativity.

Chapter 13

Sonship, discipline and kingdom authority was instilled in the sons of God from the moment they were aware of their origin, habitation and spiritual existence as sons. They had always existed in their father; each son was a member of his body, each one asserting his own strength, working in the measure allotted him as a portion of their father's spirit.

Today the sons of God would present themselves before their father, as this was a special day. Father was going to let them experience the results of creativity by their own spoken word. Father watched his sons as they came before him. He smiled, although he wanted to burst out laughing at the pushing, shoving and tumbling over one another, in playfulness, to see who would be first in line and closest to him. Momentarily he was overcome with a powerful surge of love that made him exclaim, "What a family, what love!" He loved them as his own body and he would go to any length and breadth to protect them. He would give his own life for them; his sons were his family, THE MANY MANIFESTATIONS OF HIMSELF.

The sons of God were as numerous as the stars in the heavens and in the brightness of the clearness of the sky; they looked like multitudes of clouds filling the heavens, as they accompanied their father. Sounds of voices and laughter echoed through the atmosphere as the sons called to one another like children when discovering something unique and fascinating. Before them was total darkness as they entered far into space. In the distance ahead were shimmering twinkling lights. The closer they came to the lights they recognized the galaxies their father had created. The heavens were illuminated with their brightness. The sons of God described the galaxies as roads and highways paved with golden dust and glittering stones, fit for the feet of a king and creator to walk on. They gazed in wonder at the universe about them, the stars, the planets and the darkness that stretched far beyond them. THEY WERE LITERALLY CLOTHED WITH THE UNIVERSE AND ALL IT CONTAINED, as a king literally clothed in a robe of royalty secure in his kingdom. They gazed in wonder at life surrounding them, how awesome!

Father looked at his sons while speaking softly, "My sons, the time has come for you to experience the excitement and pride of creating by your own spoken word. Remember you are my spirit; therefore, you have the same creative power in you. Come now, who will be first?" One by one the sons, who had seen their father speak the earth, sun, moon, stars and planets into existence, mimicked and imitated their father's manner

The Descent of the Sons of God (A Parable)

and confidence. They focused with wisdom on areas of darkness, speaking forth into the atmosphere, uttering creative words loudly and precisely. At each command the flickering of light would appear, slowly growing brighter, and then taking its place in the heavens becoming a new Galaxy. AT THE BIRTH OF EACH STAR the sons of God would rejoice, leaping and dancing with all of their might, their celebration was as the sound of rumbling thunder throughout the heavens. Father lovingly interrupted the celebration urging his sons to follow him, as there were nine planets in the solar system to explore and learn about. He expounded and taught his sons about time and space, far beyond the earth, far beyond the human eye's capacity to see, light years away. Father also spoke of the things of the spirit, referring to the planets he went on to say, "Only those of the spirit can see and understand the beauty of these worlds, they are a mystery yet to be revealed to the sons of men. But to you my sons, the mystery is for you to know." Again he resumed his teaching.

The sons of God marveled at the perfection of creation. They understood that the gravitational field was a force necessary for the heavenly bodies. If one heavenly body failed to stay in space, all would fail. Father created that force by his word and it would always uphold all things.

The sons of God learned many things as they spent time with their father. They commented of the fact that each body had no light of its own; it received its light from the stars and sun. They brought this to the attention of their father saying, "Father, we noticed that the planets reflect light from the greater light of

Marye Nicholas

the sun and stars. We see a pattern, we, your sons reflect the light of the greater light, your light father."

Again words failed the sons as they reverently stood at attention gazing at the sun in its strength and immensity. The intenseness of the heat was amazing. The sun was made completely of gases. The layer of the sun's atmosphere called photosphere was the part of the sun that was made up of earth-sized cells called granules. These cells constantly changed shape, carrying hot gas from the center of the sun out to the surface, and then cycled the cooler gas back to the surface to be reheated. This heat would be for the warmth of the earth. What a phenomenal sight, how stately it looked. The heavens were assuredly a tabernacle for the sun. Oh the wisdom and knowledge of father, how unsearchable are his riches and his ways past finding out, nothing was amiss, he thought of everything. The sons of God saw a pattern, a parallel. The first begotten, the Lamb of God, was the link that would hold all things together. He would uphold all things by the word of his power in heaven and in earth. As this revelation became a reality, it illuminated the minds of the sons of God. Songs of praise began to ring through the air. Some were shouting, some were weeping, some were praising, some were singing, but all bowed on their knees crying, "HOLY, HOLY, HOLY," as they worshiped their father.

The Descent of the Sons of God (A Parable)

The Heavens Could Not Contain Their Glory.

Chapter 14

What a glorious time full of wonder and awe, quality time spent together exploring the universes and galaxies far beyond the earth and its solar system. Father and his sons talked and laughed together as their presence moved through the heavens. They were bound with the bond of love: an unbreakable bond, they were one. Father beckoned to his sons to follow him; they moved through the milky ways, past Orion, Pleiades and Arcturus, retracing their path, descending into the earth's atmosphere, as the morning sun's rays glimmered and danced in the heaven. The brightness of the light expanded, reaching forth to touch its creator. As the rays of the sun gently touched father, his great light exploded into a rainbow of brilliant colors engulfing his sons. The heavens could not contain the glory of the father and his sons. No tongue, thought or words could describe the glorious beauty of their descent into the "Garden of God."

The Garden of God was a holy place, a realm of perfection. Symbolically the sons of God were as fruitful trees that produced the perfect fruits of righteousness. The production of their fruit was very evident in his garden. As father watched his sons, his thoughts went to the earth. He would take each of them, and as a tree he would plant them in the earth. He would form them tenderly under the shadow of his hand. He would shape them, as a potter shapes his vessel of beauty. He would teach them, and mold them into his image! Then he would breathe his breath of life into them and they would become a living soul, sons that he would live in.

The Garden of God would be a meeting place, a holy place, and a place of separation. In the garden everything, to the soul of man, would be new and intriguing. It would be as a child inquisitive and full of wonder. The soul of man would have to learn the things of God from the spirit. The soul of man would learn the wonderful works of God and kingdom authority. They would take the things they learned in the Garden of God into the earth and teach mankind. The sad thing was, father thought, the sons of God would not remember the garden, as it presently existed. They would only remember their transgression and their banishment from "HIS GARDEN."

Father called his sons to him and began separating them into two separate groups, one group of sons at his left and one group of sons at his right. Father called each son by his name, as they came before him, appointing them to their appointed place beside him. When he was finished his first impulse was to gather them unto himself and hold them close,

The Descent of the Sons of God (A Parable)

never to be separated. He couldn't do this and he knew it. The sons of God had to go into the earth to prepare the way for THE LAMB OF GOD. His mind was set and his plan had to be accomplished.

A river of life flowed out of Eden into the GARDEN OF GOD. The river watered the garden, giving life to every tree and plant enclosed within it. From the Garden of God, the river of life went into the earth, multiplying into four bodies of water that would supply water to the four corners of the earth. Father rose to his feet and walked to the banks of the river. He strolled up and down in deep thought; his mind was on the future of his sons. In a sense he was giving his sons as an offering for his plan to be accomplished. They were a sweet smelling savor to him; in fact, the abundance of their life permeated the air as incense, as a fragrant offering to him.

The sound of laughter brought him back to the present. He always felt a quickening in his inner being when his sons laughed. Their laughter was like a beautiful melody to his ears that never ceased. He was deeply stirred and he spoke softly to himself in a low tone, "I love you my sons, I love you, I love you!"

Turning to face his children he spoke clearly and precisely. "I have separated you into two groups for a reason. One group will stay for an appointed time; the other group that I have chosen will go into the earth. My sons, you are now aware of the Lamb of God, the first begotten son, WHO WILL BE OFFERED ON A CROSS AS A SACRIFICE FOR THE SINS OF THE SONS OF MEN. He will give his life to bring you, my sons, back to me. The glory you now have, he will return to you, so you can take your place in me once again, forever. He is in me and I am in him. We are one, as you my sons are one in me and I in you. THE LAMB OF GOD, THE SON OF GOD will come back into me when his work is finished; for you see my sons, when you see me you see him, when you see him you see me. To put it in words that you can understand; THE LAMB OF GOD will be your door, your way back to me!"

Addressing the first group of sons he explained to them that they would be the first to go into the earth. He went on to say, "You will walk in darkness and dwell in the land of the shadow of death, but upon you the light shall shine. Unto you a child will be born, unto you my sons, a son shall be given. The government shall be upon his shoulders. His name shall be called WONDERFUL, COUNSELOR, THE MIGHTY GOD, THE EVERLASTING FATHER, THE PRINCE OF PEACE. THEN, AFTER THE CROSS, THE SECOND GROUP OF SONS SHALL GO INTO THE EARTH. He shall be your example and make it possible for you to be as he is, and eventually to live in immortality, immortal sons of God. He is the Good Shepherd, the door to the fold, the way, the truth, and the light and life of man." Pausing for a moment he asks, "Do you remember the parable of the prodigal son?" The sons nodded in affirmation. Pointing to the first group of sons he said, "You are the prodigal son. Through the sacrifice of the fatted calf, the LAMB OF GOD, you will be forgiven and restored."

Addressing the second group of sons he explained, "You are the brother that stayed at home. There will be times you will question why man transgressed and wasted his inheritance, causing all men to fall short of the glory of the father. One day you will understand

The Descent of the Sons of God (A Parable)

and celebrate with me their return. Everything in the heaven above, and in the earth, and on the earth; new worlds, far into eternity as the universes multiply and expand, at an appointed time, when my words are fulfilled, you will reign with me." The faces of the sons glowed with excitement. They now understood the plan and saw the vision of their father and the vision of the salvation and redemption of mankind. They would be his dwelling place, his tabernacle. When their glory was restored they would return to him and there would be a glorious feast of all his tabernacles. All of the sons of God jumped to their feet leaping and shouting, "Father is love, father is love, father is love! He loves us so much he planned our redemption and salvation before he created the earth." The adoration, praise and worship lasted for a long period of time, as their father stood in the midst of them dwelling in their praises. As their voices became silent they knew, without a shadow of doubt, that they had been chosen to prepare the way for the FIRST BEGOTTEN SON OF GOD, who was in the bosom of their father. They fully accepted their responsibilities as sons. Here and now, they knew who they were and where they were going, accepting their destiny.

It was time to leave. The first group of sons stood to their feet once more. For the last time they would present themselves before their father, embrace their brothers and go into the earth. One by one the sons came before him. He spoke their names softly and embraced them. The brothers that would stay wept aloud as they watched their brethren say goodbye to their father. Some bowed on their knees with their face in their hands weeping. Others buried their faces in their father's lap sobbing, while others lay prostrate on the ground before him calling his name. Father could hardly speak; heart-rending emotion was seen in his eyes. "I love you, I love you my sons; you are my beloved ones, my beloved sons. I promise you I will always be with you, I will never leave or forsake you." His voice broke, father wept.

Time had come, a silence hung over the GARDEN OF GOD as father walked among his sons. "I must choose one from among you that will go ahead of you. He will be first to descend into the earth and you will follow thereafter," father said. "He will be the husbandman, a leader, a watchman, and a High Priest. He will lead, instruct and carefully guide his brethren. He will watch over them to make sure they, as the trees in my garden, are fruitful and prosperous." Carefully he scanned through the sons and his eyes met the eyes of ADAM. "ADAM, COME TO ME," FATHER CALLED. FATHER PLACED HIS HANDS UPON ADAM'S HEAD SAYING, "I BLESS YOU WITH ALL AUTHORITY IN THE EARTH. When you have learned to rule well, you will rule the heavens and the earth. Every thing will be made subject to you. As time passes, corporeally you and your brothers will be called the Adamic Race, the first Adam. Remember my son, I have made provisions for you to return to me, I love you Adam. Are you ready?" All eyes were on the father and his son as Adam stepped forward. "Yes father," he replied, "I am ready." Father embraced him holding him close for a moment, looking deep into his eyes he said, "I WILL WAIT FOR YOUR RETURN." TOGETHER THEY WALKED TO THE BANK OF THE RIVER OF LIFE. Hand in hand they descended into the earth.

The Descent of the Sons of God (A Parable)

SCRIPTURE REFERENCES FOR THE "PARABLE"

Day unto day – Psalms 19:2
Laid the foundations of the earth – Job 38:4
Crowned with glory and honor – Psalms 8:5
Rode upon the wings of the wind – Psalms 18:10
Lift up your heads oh ye gates – Psalms 24:7
Command the morning and let the Dayspring – Job 38:12
I have formed it to be inhabited – Isaiah 45:18
Walked in search of the deep – Job 38:16
From everlasting to everlasting – Psalms 90:2
Before the mountains you were – Proverbs 8.25
No height or death can separate us – Romans 8:34
Paved work of sapphire – Exodus 24th Chapter
Right hand spanned the heavens – Isaiah 29:46
Trees clapped their hands – Isaiah 55:12
Hills skipped like lambs – Psalms 114:4
Righteousness and peace kissed each other – Psalms 85:10
Sit on the circle of the earth – Isaiah 40:22
I have measured the waters – Isaiah 40:12
Ask me concerning my works – Isaiah 45:11
The Lord is my shepherd – Psalms 24
Jesus' crucifixion – Psalms 22
Brightness of my glory – Hebrews 1:3
A smoke went up from his nostrils – Psalms 18:8
Loose those that are appointed to death – Psalms 102:20

Marye Nicholas

I will declare your name to my brethren – Psalms 22:22
As a garment you will fold them up – Hebrews 1:12
Shut up the places with bars – Job 38
Fastened the earth and laid the corner stone – Job 38
The chambers of his house in the midst of it – Psalms 104:3
Praise him with a timbrel Psalms – 149:3
Alpha and Omega, Ancient of Days – Daniel 7
The Holy City – Revelations 21
Walls of salvation anal gates of praise – Isaiah 26:1
All things by the word of his power – Hebrews 1:3
The riches of the wisdom and knowledge – Romans 11:33
God is my portion – Psalms 119:57
Opened the river in high places – Isaiah 41:11
The garden east in Eden – Genesis 3

THE DESCENT OF THE SONS OF GOD

A PARABLE

TEACHING

BY MARYE NICHOLAS

PART TWO

Marye Nicholas

The Descent of the Sons of God (A Parable)

"ACCORDING AS HE HAS CHOSEN US IN HIM BEFORE THE FOUNDATIONS OF THE WORLD: THAT WE SHOULD BE HOLY AND WITHOUT BLAME BEFORE HIM IN LOVE." (EPH. 1:4)

Chapter 1

For years I have heard the scriptures that God had chosen us in him before the foundations of the world. I quoted it over and over never really knowing what I was saying. "In him, hallelujah" "I'm in him, glory!" I think back trying to recall what I meant when I quoted this scripture, possibly seeing myself hidden in him, which is scriptural, but not applicable to this particular passage.

One morning in 2001 during my prayer time, I was caught up in the spirit realm. I saw my father moving through the heavens, far beyond and before the universe, solar system, sun, moon, stars and our earth were ever created. I literally heard the words of his mouth and saw the evidence of his utterance become products of his creative faith.

Marye Nicholas

I saw many sons without number, within the magnificence of his splendor, and as each son stood amazed, his word produced galaxies, universes and worlds. The sons would shout loudly and rejoice as they looked into the vastness of space without time, with the inquisitiveness of children anticipating the next wonder of his majestic work. To my surprise and delight as I looked closer, I saw myself among the sons who were wide-eyed and innocent; loving each moment of adventure, with their father of love. Within that realm of love, the heavens rang with laughter, joyous exclamations of praise continually burst forth as an aroma of sweet smelling incense. We, as sons of God, being in our father, were each a part of our father. Everything he did creatively, we were a part of, rejoicing and delighting in him eternally. We were his delight and the very substance of his eternal spirit of life. Our existence was in him; we were placed in him as sons of his being and likeness. (Ye are Gods – Psalms 82:6) in Eph. 1:5 the scripture states, "having predestinated us into the adoption (placement) of sons (children) by Jesus Christ to himself, according to the good pleasure of his will." It was always his will to reinstate us. We were predestinated before the transgression to be placed back into him, through the resurrection and the finished work of Jesus Christ.

All of the wonders I experienced in the spirit realm had taken place before we descended to be formed in the earth, and of the earth. We were made to know the power of praise as sons before creation. We were taught to function and focus in the perimeter of his mind and to never be outside of him or his presence. Before Adam sinned he began to separate

The Descent of the Sons of God (A Parable)

himself mentally from his father. He stepped out of the unity and oneness with his spirit, and the spirit of his father. The glory and honor that Adam was crowned with no longer existed, the light of his temple had gone out, the righteousness of his father had been removed because he had followed the dictates of his soul.

Before we left our father to come into the earth, he pronounced blessings over us. He spoke forth good things like: grace, favor, richness of knowledge and wealth. The greatest blessing would be the fullness of the Godhead bodily, which would come through Jesus; yet was in Adam, who was to be the pattern of Jesus, and Jesus the pattern of GOD. All of this was determined in advance before the foundation of the earth, and we were sealed as Sons of God in him. We were sealed with the HOLY SPIRIT *AND* A HOLY SPIRIT, confirming our sonship, as father no longer looked on the flesh and the offense of the flesh. Therefore the sons were returned to their glory. All this was done in the beloved, so that he might gather together in one all things in Christ, both in heaven and in earth, EVEN IN HIM. That "even in him" is, *we*, (you and me) the Sons of God. PRAISE THE LORD! God had a plan. He took substance of himself and made a family of sons without number, so that he could be manifested as God in men. God in a human body with a pure, just, innocent and righteous mind to rule in the earth and eventually in the heavens; to be all that he was, superior to any creature that was ever created. GOD AND MAN IN A HUMAN BODY.

Marye Nicholas

The Descent of the Sons of God (A Parable)

Chapter 2

OOPS, there was a problem; the soul was not spirit and could never understand the things of the spirit, or know the things of the spirit. Why? THE SOUL HAD A MIND OF ITS OWN! The spirit of man had been with father (THE ANCIENT OF DAYS FOR-EVER.) The spirit of man had seen first hand the magnificence of their father's love and glory. Isaiah said: "I saw the Lord sitting upon a throne, high and lifted up, and his train filled the temple." (Isaiah 6-1) CHILDREN, we were and are clothed in him., we were clothed with his glory. His many sons were AND ARE the train of glory that fills father's temple. We were and are his spiritual image, taken from within him, with every attribute and characteristic: "he that has seen me, has seen the father" (John 14:8).

If ADAM HAD COME THROUGH WITH FLYING COLORS HE WOULD HAVE ENTERED INTO A HIGHER LEVEL. The garden was east in Eden. Could Eden be another spiritual level? Could it be possible that there is a comparison to the levels or stages of the temple in the Old Testament? Could the earth be the OUTER COURT and the GARDEN the HOLY PLACE? What about EDEN, was it the HOLY OF HOLIES? IF THIS WAS TRUE, Adam never made it into the HOLY OF HOLIES. If he had, I believe, he would have remembered his origin? Jesus said, "I know whence I came, and whither I go" (John 8:14) It didn't happen that way; he would never reach the goal. He would miss the mark. SYMBOLICALLY, HE WENT INTO THE OUTER COURT, never fulfilling his potential as a Son of God.

IN THE BEGINNING the spirit and soul were one, the soul of man was innocent, interacting with the spirit. The soul walked in the same level of the spirit. The soul of Adam begins to accept the glory of its spirit as its own; after the transgression, the soul couldn't remain in the realm of the spirit. The spirit realm was no longer accessible to the spirit, soul or body.

NOW VISUALIZE THIS; a spirit being, with a soul, that was like an innocent curious child, who was the bearer of light, the light of its spirit. The soul and body would be the vehicle of the spirit, expressing its glory. The soul would be like a proud Olympic runner, carrying the torch. On the sidelines spectators urge him on and encourage the runner, while others begin to applaud and whistle. The light bearer begins to accept the applause and glory for himself, forgetting the purpose of his performance. The purpose was lost in the vanity of the moment.

Adam's soul BEGAN ACCEPTING THE GLORY OF ITS SPIRIT AS ITS OWN, THEREBY separating itself from the oneness and unity with its father.

The Descent of the Sons of God (A Parable)

In the first chapter of the parable, I mention the family of God in great detail. The family began in father; the idea of the family came from him. Man didn't invent the family or the idea of family; we came from the loins of our father, as Levi was in the loins of Abraham when he paid tithes to Melchizedek. In his likeness, we were spawned from the loins of our father, enjoying and expressing all of his emotions of laughter and love. We were joyfully and hilariously in love with him; daily in his presence acting just like him.

I want to open your understanding and stretch your imagination. Picture in your mind a mother who is very large with child. Everywhere that mother goes, that child goes with her. As she shops, as she walks, and as she goes about her daily routine, that child in her tummy stays right with her, it is a part of her. Now, let's go one step further. Each child she conceives is a substance of her and has a part of her in it. All of her children make up the mother and the father, each child is a portion of the parents. Eventually the parents will be limited in their childbearing as they grow older, but father is infinite; he breathes his spirit into man and from that time on, at each birth, a spirit is birthed out of the spirit realm into a human being, until an appointed time. I began in him and my origin is in him. Everywhere he went I was right there with him. David said, "The lord does ride on the wings of the wind (spirit) and on a cherub he does fly. Twenty thousand are his great chariots and thousands of angels on high." (Psalms 68:17) In the Tenach, page 1493, the Hebrew reads, "God's entourage is twice ten thousand and thousands of angels. The lord is among them."

Marye Nicholas

CHILDREN, SINCE I WAS IN HIM BEFORE EARTH-TIME EVER EXISTED, I RODE UPON THE WINGS OF THE WIND WITH HIM, AND SAT UPON THE CIRCLE OF THE EARTH, LAUGHING AND REJOICING AND DELIGHTING IN HIM; WHILE STANDING IN AWE OF THE WONDERS AND SPLENDOR OF HIS WORKMANSHIP.

The Descent of the Sons of God (A Parable)

Chapter 3

"And the youngest of them said to his father, father give me the portion of goods that befalleth to me. And he divided unto them his living." (Luke 15-12) I read a book written by an infamous minister who had a dream about spirits, in the spirit realm, which were anxious to come to the earth. They would plead with father to let them go each time a baby was birthed. When the prodigal son asked for his inheritance, it wasn't that he was in strife with his father, or had sibling rivalry with his brother; he wanted to go into the world to make a difference and make his mark in the earth.

The prodigal loved his father and brother, they were his family, but he wanted to travel, explore and have his own friends and vocation. All of this was exciting and appealing and would have worked had the son kept the laws, principles and precepts of his father. You see distance had nothing to do with his desires and decisions. He had been taught truth and uprightness, ruler-ship and authority, everything that would be necessary to start a new life in a new place. All of the son's life he had walked in his father's footsteps, until you could no longer tell the father's footsteps and footprints from the son's. Everything the father had, was, and would ever be, was placed within his sons. When the younger son left home he was equipped with everything he would ever need: word power, authority, wisdom, knowledge, kingship and creative abilities; plus, he knew how to function in each. The younger son made himself comfortable in his new environment. He began to set up his life, vineyard and garden. Outside of his garden there was a different atmosphere than what he was used to, encompassing him and infiltrating his mind (soul). There were many voices, adversaries (serpents) instructing, whispering and hissing in his ear. He was caught up with the attention and the flattery of self-acclaimed friends. He begins to listen and to see himself as the voices described he would be, not what he really was; a true son who had wealth, a son that could bear the responsibility of investing wisely, increasing his father's investment which had been invested in him. There is an old saying, "hindsight is better than foresight." Later in his life the young son would look back and see that he should have sought the advice and counsel of others, experts in their business, vineyard and gardens. He would have multiplied his wealth, whereas he could have poured out his wealth and blessings on others. Eventually the son's eyes were opened to the betrayal of his friends. It was too late to salvage his goods and start over. He had no excuse, or pride, he was so ashamed. He had lost his vineyard and garden that he had neglected, and wasted his inheritance that his father had invested in him; of his own will and

The Descent of the Sons of God (A Parable)

rebellion he was driven out penniless. In his frustrations he hired himself out to another and was placed in a position of the lowest degree. As Adam, he was driven into the earth (soulish realm) into the very dust of the earth. Talk about low, you can't get any lower than that. He desired to eat the husks that the swine consumed, husks that come from an ear of corn, and corn comes from the earth, grown in the dirt of the earth. It sounds to me like the soul was on the same level as the serpent, adversary and whisperer. David said in the Psalms, "You have brought me to the dust of death." (Psalms 22:15) "For our soul is bowed down to the dust: our belly cleaves to the dust of the earth." (Psalms 44:25) The unrenewed soul or mind, reasons and fluctuates and covenants with death. Praise the lord for the father, who had never stopped looking for his son, but instead was waiting for him to return. Think on this children, our father knew, when he sent his sons into the earth, that they would return. Why? He had ordained it. He was a father of his word, his sons would never remain in an incomplete state, he would bring them into perfection. Knowing this, he waited patiently for them.

It is amazing that the son's father knew him from afar, when countless people had traveled up and down that road daily. Not one time did the father drop everything and begin to run. When the father told his servants to get the robe, ring and shoes, he didn't tell them to look in the basement in a box in the closet. No! He had the robe, ring and shoes laid out just as the son had left them. The father was getting ready to reinstate his son. He had never entertained the thought to discard or replace him with another. He had predestined this before his sons were born. They were a part of him. Nicodemus questioned Jesus, asking him, how a man could be born again. Could he go back into the mother's womb? (John 3:1) I say, can he go back into his father's loins? No! You cannot un-birth a baby! WHEN THE PRODIGAL'S FATHER caught hold of his son, the spirit of the son witnessed with the spirit of his father crying, "ABBA, FATHER!" THE FATHER RETURNING AND AFFIRMING THE CRY, "MY SON, MY SON!"

On the day of Pentecost, Jesus had been resurrected (passed over into the spirit realm to return to his power and authority he had before the foundations of the world were created). He took his throne as "THE MOST HIGH GOD," KEEPING HIS PROMISE TO RETURN HIS BRETHREN TO THEIR GLORY, BY GIVING THEM HIS GLORY, AS INDIVIDUAL SONS AND A CORPORATE SON. Something was getting ready to happen. A manifestation, a revealing, a new order had taken place in the spirit realm and now would come with a great force into the earth. As the glory of God filled the tabernacle of Moses, (2nd Chronicles 5:13-14) and filled Solomon's temple, until there was no room for man; so also the glory of God was getting ready to enter into the spirit of man. A change of order was taking place; the spirit of man would be the TEMPLE OF THE LIVING GOD, JUST AS IT WAS BEFORE THE TRANSGRESSION OF ADAM. The second chapter of Acts speaks of when the day of Pentecost was FULLY COME, WHEN THE APPOINTED TIME had come, a time chosen out of eternity, that time, that day, that particular moment had arrived, there came a sound, a noise that had never been

The Descent of the Sons of God (A Parable)

heard before, as of a rushing, forceful strong wind, (spirit) a spiritual force like a wind entered the place where they were sitting. I don't know about you but I believe since the day of Pentecost was fully come; knowing this, the people in Jerusalem would be congregated wall to wall in the temple. That is why there was such a commotion. This would be the appropriate place to change the order of things. The old earthly temple would no longer be recognized as the house and dwelling place for God to dwell among his people. That mighty rushing wind (spirit) the spirit of holiness entered into the spirits of men, reconciling them to father once more. GOD AND MAN, MAN AND GOD: A NEW TEMPLE FOR THEIR FATHER TO DWELL IN AND LIVE IN.

There is a passage of scripture in 1st Kings 1:39 that comes close to explaining a transfer of power, not unlike the day of Pentecost. King David had given his word that his son Solomon would ascend his throne as the next king. "And Zadok the priest took a horn of oil out of the tabernacle and anointed Solomon and they blew the trumpet; and all the people said, God save King Solomon. And all the people came up after him, and the people piped with pipes, and rejoiced with great joy, so that the earth rent, broke asunder, apart, with the sound of their voices, music and praise. This sound reverberated as thunder, as a great earthquake breaking and shaking the earth. In comparison, Jesus had just been crowned KING OF KINGS AND LORD OF LORDS and he was letting it be known. Why be silent about it, let the world know that the realm of the spirit is open once again to man, made accessible by the LAST ADAM, THE LORD JESUS CHRIST, who fulfilled the law and redeemed mankind. The heaven and the earth were affected by the transference of power and the new creation of man. When the spirit of God swept through the temple, Jerusalem, earth and spirit realm; a loving and forgiving father embraced his many sons, lifting them once again above the earth into the heavenlies. The Sons of God now receiving their glory, are raising their faces and voices in praise crying, "ABBA FATHER!"

Children, I can see it now. When he took captivity captive, taking his brethren back to the father, the fatted calf had already been sacrificed. They, also, becoming the temple of the HOLY SPIRIT, were now feasting, dancing and rejoicing "in him." I can see in my mind, my father looking into the face of the KING OF KINGS saying, "It looks like the feast of the tabernacles to me son," and they begin to rejoice.

The Descent of the Sons of God (A Parable)

Chapter 4

In a meeting in Tulsa, Oklahoma I heard a minister say, "I have heard this message that I am going to preach, taught and interpreted in different ways. As you and I know there are more sides to a mountain than one and many ways to climb that mountain; this is my way." In the parable I spoke about the younger son as an example of Adam, the person of Adam and the corporate Adam. Adam until the fall, and then from the fall to the cross, after the transgression, begins to descend into depravity, into the dust of humanity, being ruled by their flesh, carnal mind and emotions. The corporate elder son (the first shall be last and the last shall be first) stayed at home with his father. He would be birthed into the earth after the cross. ALL would come through the door that Jesus prepared for us before the foundations of the earth were placed in the heavens. ALL were made righteous, as, ALL THROUGH JESUS FULFILLED THE LAW and were sealed with the HOLY SPIRIT of promise as SONS. When I say ALL, that ALL includes those also before the cross. (Romans 8:3-4)

Back in the heavenlies a feast was going on before the Lamb of God was slain. Those in the father; in the spirit realm, begin to rejoice and be merry. The appointed time was near. The robe, shoes and the ring were ready. In fact they had been ready since the younger son had left home.

In the earth the father had appointed sons to prepare the way of JESUS, THE WAY, THE DOOR; TO LEAD HIS BRETHREN BACK INTO THE FATHER. Simeon and Anna were waiting in the temple. Zacharias, Elizabeth, Mary, Joseph, John the Baptist, Disciples that had been with him for three and a half years and countless others would be those sons that prepared his way so they could enter, JESUS *THE* DOOR, back into their father.

We who came after the cross, that were still in him, not as yet birthed into this earth, were the other son, have had a tendency to point our finger at the younger son saying, "If it wasn't for Adam's rebellion and transgression, we would be living in a paradise and everything would be perfect. When I get to heaven I'm going to tell him what I think about his usurping the authority of God, I would never had done that." (Famous last words) We SHOULD BE FEASTING AND REJOICING! JESUS WAS IN FATHER, RECONCILING MAN UNTO HIM, MAKING GOD AND MAN ONE, WITH ONE SPIRIT.

The First Begotten from the dead took away the offense of the flesh, returning the sons to the glory we had in eternity before our time began on earth. I can hear my father who had waited for thousands of years to feast once again with his sons lovingly say, "Everything I have is yours, everything I am is in you,

The Descent of the Sons of God (A Parable)

and all you have to do is take possession of it. Adam sinned and fell short of my glory and the glory I had given man and crowned him with. If the Lamb of God had not been sacrificed, you would have come into the world without hope. My corporate son was dead but now he is alive. He is dressed again as royalty. Let the feast of the tabernacles begin!"

Marye Nicholas

The Descent of the Sons of God (A Parable)

Chapter 5

THE DOOR (ST. JOHN 10th Chapter)
"Verily, verily, I say unto you; unless you walk through the door of the sheepfold: you will be judged as a thief that steals, plunders and scatters the sheep by force." This is an unconditional statement that Jesus said; you can't climb, rise up in fame and fortune, or go through the priesthood, Abraham or Moses to get into the sheepfold. You have to come in one way. That way is through the door. I AM THE SHEPHERD OF THE SHEEP AND I HAVE TO ENTER IN BY THE DOOR. I am the door of the sheep, not only the door of the sheep, but of the fold.

God himself would have to come through Jesus, and as Jesus, to become the door. Jesus would have to go through that door, to become that door. Being the door to the fold and the door to the sheep, he was the first son to ENTER AS THE NEW SPECIES, GOD AND MAN, INTO THE FOLD. "And when he puts forth his own sheep he goes before them and his sheep will follow him because they know his voice." HOW

Marye Nicholas

DID HE GO BEFORE THEM? Before the foundations of the earth existed, Jesus was in the bosom of the father waiting for the appointed time to leave the fold. The fold was the bosom of the father and this fold was and would be the fold for mankind, his sheep. The first time Jesus stepped out of the fold to lead his sheep, was with Adam; Jesus was the TREE OF LIFE in the garden. Adam was taken out of Jesus, out of the bosom of father and placed in a garden or realm, where he could go in and out of this realm. He put forth Adam as an individual and as the corporate Adam. He went before them through Noah, Abraham, Moses, the Priesthood, the ARK OF THE COVANANT, the cloud by day and the fire by night. His spirit spoke through the prophets declaring and proclaiming his word; the word was his law and his word was his voice.

Throughout the Old Testament Israel was portrayed as scattered sheep. The shepherds were as hirelings. They were more interested in wages than concern for the sheep. The Priesthood, Pharisees, and Sadducees, were wounding the sheep and then would not heal the wound. They were trying to take the kingdom by violence, they were trying to get into the fold the wrong way. The only way to enter the fold was through Jesus. Jesus said the sheep knew his voice and he called them by their name. Their name is their identity and nature. Before the foundations of the earth, they were in him. Jesus said of his disciples in his prayer to his father, "They are not of this world as I am not of this world." (John 15:19,17:14) "If ye had known me, ye should have known my father ALSO; henceforth ye know him and have seen him." The disciples were being told, you know me sons, because I

The Descent of the Sons of God (A Parable)

am the father, you were in me before the foundations of the earth were created. Children, I am telling you, father knew his children, they were made in his image, identity and nature, but they had all fallen short of his glory. Their spirits never forgot who they were, but the mind could not remember.

"And Mary arose in those days, and went into the hill country with haste, into a city of Judah; and entered into the house of Zacharias and saluted Elisabeth. And it carne to pass, that when Elisabeth heard the salutation of Mary, the babe leaped in her womb; and Elisabeth was filled with the HOLY GHOST." A few moments later Elisabeth would say, "For lo, as soon as the voice of the salutation sounded in mine ears, the babe leaped in my womb for joy." (Luke 1:39) The spirit of baby John recognized the spirit of baby Jesus and leaped for joy because he recognized his creator. He knew him, for he had been in him.

Jesus became the door for the sheep into the fold. He gave all sheep access through him; those on earth and those still in the spirit realm, and also those in father that have not been birthed in the earth as new creatures in CHRIST JESUS. ALL IN HEAVEN AND EARTH WOULD HAVE TO COME THROUGH JESUS. HIS SHEEP WOULD HAVE ONE FOLD, AS IT WAS IN TIME WITHOUT END. ALL OF HIS SONS WILL TAKE THEIR PLACES WITH HIS IMAGE AND IDENTITY IN ONE FOLD; IN THE BOSOM OF THE FATHER.

Marye Nicholas

The Descent of the Sons of God (A Parable)

Chapter 6

The Spirit Realm is Real:
My first encounter with the spirit realm was at the age of five where my daddy pastored a denominational church in Council Bluff, Iowa. As a small child I had always been aware of the presence of the Lord. I would talk with him and daydream of him daily: singing, laughing and dancing before him in my childish innocence. I had noticed at night when the lights were out, that a couple of hours later, a being of small stature would peer in the screen door at me.

In the days of my childhood, there were not too many pastors that could pick or choose their parsonage. They had to take what came along with the territory. There were two rooms and a kitchen, and at night my sister and I had the privilege of sleeping on a couch that folded into a bed in the living room. One night as I lay thinking and listening to night sounds like dogs barking, or people in the distance laughing and talking, I saw a small figure come up the steps to the screen door. When I say small, I mean three feet tall and not an inch more. He put his face up to the screen, cupped his hands over

Marye Nicholas

his eyes, so as to focus on something in particular, evidently that something was yours truly. His eyes searched the room and fell on me. He stared at me for a few minutes, which seemed like thirty, then he moved away from the door and left. This scenario repeated itself again the following night. The third evening, my daddy, who was not aware of what was happening, decided to sleep in the room with my sister and I. The lights were turned out and everyone was asleep. As I lay there I thought of the previous evenings and couldn't get the scene out of my mind. I was so nervous and scared that I looked around the room for some place to hide. With any luck, daddy would hear me moving around and scold me if he saw me hiding under something. I guess I would take my chances. Around midnight, just like clockwork, the little being appeared. I sat up in my bed so terrified that I couldn't talk or scream. He opened the screen door and stepped into the doorway, when all of a sudden a thunderous voice boomed out, "Here! What are you doing?" THE FIGURE JUMPED OUT OF THE DOOR, DOWN THE STEPS, ONTO THE SIDEWALK AND DIS-APPEARED. Daddy was never aware of what had taken place; he had called out in his sleep because he had heard a noise. I know my heavenly father had protected me that night and it drew me much closer to the reality of the spirit realm. I don't believe it was a human being, nor was I dreaming or imagining. It was real to me as a child of five. EVIL HAS MANY FORMS. I BELIEVE IT MANIFESTED ITSELF TO A CHILD AND THIS CHILD WAS DELIVERED FROM EVIL THAT NIGHT.

The Descent of the Sons of God (A Parable)

At seven years of age I received my awareness of sonship, realizing I was reconciled to my father, therefore I made a decision to abandon myself to him. When I received my spiritual language at eight years of age I was caught up in the realm of the spirit. "I saw the Lord high and lifted up and his train filled the temple." When I came to myself, I was speaking in my heavenly language. Later in my life when I left home on my own, I didn't always stay in that glory realm I experienced as a child. I have learned not to look back and say, "Look at all the times you missed it." Now I look back and say, "Look at the stairs you have climbed!" Each error, accidentally, or intentionally has been an experience in my humanity: a step upward, not a step downward. I am being formed, molded and squeezed as clay into shape: into the stature of the Lord Jesus Christ, the Son of God, into a perfect man. (Eph 4:13) Trials and tribulations are for the forming of the Sons of God. Testings are not for the spirit man; testings are for the soulish man, the soul, your soul. I suppose great tribulations come to those who are more rebellious and unrelenting.

Salvation is for the soul. When the soul is taught the word and begins to be obedient to the word and becomes submissive to the word and the soul becomes submissive to its spirit; I believe the transformation will come. FULL GROWN SONS OF GOD! This is the mystery Paul was speaking about, of Christ and the church. REMEMBER, the spirit has received its glory; the soul is being saved.

Accessing spiritual encounters:

In my study time I mentally went through the Old and New Testament, beginning with Genesis to

Marye Nicholas

Exodus, thinking of all of the people that had been visited by God, angels, visions and dreams. I wrote down several names of people down through the generations, in the Old and New Testament that had spiritual or supernatural encounters. In some examples, I will give the Hebrew translation from the *Tanach The Writings Of The Prophets: The Stone Addition*. Genesis 3:8 "And they (Adam and Eve) heard the voice of the Lord God walking in the garden in the cool of the day." *Tanach,* page 7, in the Hebrew translation: "They (Adam and Eve) heard the sound of Hashem (God) manifesting itself in the garden, toward evening." Before I go any further I want to explain why angels made visitations to men and why they were used by God to instruct, take charge of and keep vigil over man. When Adam and Eve sinned, they were driven out of the garden realm, a place separated, or a separated place, where they met and interacted with their father one on one. They knew him and communed with him intimately. At a particular time of the day they knew he would call to them, or they would hear his sound, movement or voice, as he came to fellowship with his children. For example, we as sons, who have intimate fellowship hear his voice, feel the moving of the spirit, our spirit as it communes with us and leads us, we become familiar with the ways of our father through our spirit. Genesis 3:24 "So he drove out the man and placed at the east of the garden of Eden, Cherubim and a flaming sword which turns every way to keep the way of the tree of life." The angel, or the Cherubim, or invisible being, would have authority over man. Because of the sin of man, he would never have access to the spirit realm, he would

The Descent of the Sons of God (A Parable)

never find his way back to the garden, until the last Adam, the Messiah, the Christ, would come and redeem him, therefore, the angel would guard that realm until the cross and the redemption. The fiery sword represented the fact that, the only way to enter the realm of the spirit was to fulfill the law. To fulfill the law, one must be sinless, perfect, or God himself. Man could not qualify. Approximately 2,000 years later, Moses was given a pattern of the tabernacle in the wilderness and was instructed carefully and precisely on how to build it. Woven into the curtains or the veil that was placed before the Most Holy Place were two cherubim, which signified once again, angels overlooking and guarding the spirit realm where God resided. When Jesus, the perfect man, the last Adam fulfilled the law, the veil was rent from the top to the bottom. Romans 8:4 says, God judged sin in the flesh, replacing it with his righteousness and holiness, that we could fulfill the law and once again have access to father, through the spirit.

Genesis 6:8, "Noah found grace in the eyes of God." "And God said to Noah." Noah heard the voice of God, he instructed him on the building of the ark. Step by step he pointed out specifically what he was to do. Through his obedience, he and his seed would be the new generation. The ark would be symbolically the womb of God and the womb of the spirit. Inside that ark was the new seed, a new creation, exactly as everything that was created was in him, father, before the foundations of the earth were laid. All life that would be placed in the earth was in the womb of the spirit. In the womb of the ark were beasts, animals and fowls, plus the food they would eat. When God told him to take the food he would eat, then Noah would take small tree sprouts, vegetation, herbs and seed. The whole scenario was representative of recreation, the new birth. The dove, the Holy Spirit moving upon the face of the deep, to bring new life, a new beginning. I honestly believe as the Spirit moved over the face of the deep, before creation, it was representative of the dove that Noah sent forth from the ark. It would hover over the earth, and then it would go back to Noah. Noah would reach forth his hand and take the dove back into the ark. When life began to appear and blossom, after the water receded, the Spirit (dove), remained in the earth. This says to me, the Spirit will always remain, or dwell in the earth.

    Abraham and Sarah's transformation physically was supernatural. Hebrews 11:11-12 the scriptures inform us that Abraham's body was as good as dead. He was one hundred years old and Sarah was ninety years old. Their physical bodies had to change, because life produces life. I am talking spiritual reality; they entered into the realm of the spirit, a new thing was happening, the super and the natural came together so that the seed could come forth. It was after they experienced the realm of the supernatural and saw what happened to them physically, that they began looking for a city, a country whose maker and founder was God. They had stepped over into that city and from that moment forth, set their minds as Paul, on the goal, and were determined to find it. Evidently they enjoyed several years of the effects of that realm, as Sarah nursed and weaned Isaac, delighting in her blessing of motherhood. After her death, Abraham remarried, fathering six more sons.

The Descent of the Sons of God (A Parable)

Several years ago I sat under the teaching of a dear friend of mine Jim Lockmiller. Being a baby to the Kingdom message, I struggled with the word I was hearing. One night I had a dream. In the dream I saw Jim in a circle and around him were small children, I was one of the children. Suddenly I saw the heavens vast and empty before me. Luminous and in all her glory the planet earth appeared, yet, there was a horizontal line of division between the heavens and the earth. As a wide-eyed child full of curiosity, I looked in wonder at the scene before me. I heard a voice say to me, "Listen to what Jim is teaching, he will bring the heavens and the earth together for you." In other words he will bring the natural and the spiritual together through the word. Then the VOICE ADDRESSED ME SAYING, "When you fully understand, then you can teach, and with the word, bring the natural and the spiritual together." It took years for me to understand, but when understanding came, it was as if it opened to me all at once. The realm of the spirit is experienced in different levels. It is like climbing stairs or climbing a ladder that reaches from heaven to the earth, we have a choice, we can ascend or descend, or we can do both and bring the natural and the supernatural together and live in the spiritual.

Exodus 3:2 reads, "And the angel of the Lord appeared unto Moses, in a flame of fire out of the midst of a bush." In Exodus 24:12, Moses went up into the mountain to receive the law, written by the finger of God. Forty days in the mountain with God began to change Moses physically, which when you remember the words of David, you will understand, "The entrance of thy word gives light." (Psalms 119:130)

Moses was in the presence of God, who is light, and transformation began to take place. Later, Moses would ask the Lord if he could see his glory. God granted that request approximately two thousand years later when Jesus was on the mount of transfiguration. The same God that gave the commandants and gave the law was the word of God and the GLORY OF GOD. Moses saw that Glory, the Son of God. God gave Moses his word, he fulfilled his word, and he became his word.

There are many more I can mention, such as, David who saw the destroying angel, Isaiah saw the Lord high and lifted up and his train filled the temple, and Daniel saw the ancient of days and the Son of God in a vision generations before the actual appearing of Jesus, the Messiah. He also saw him in another dimension after his resurrection, given his kingdom, with power and dominion.

HERE COMES JESUS! He is heralding the good news that the kingdom of heaven was at hand. He also declares that the kingdom of God in you. He is ministered to, by angels after his forty day fast, but what really impresses me, DANIEL TOLD ABOUT HIS ASCENSION, HIS ENTHRONEMENT AND HIS KINGDOM THAT WAS SET UP ON THE EARTH DURING THE ROMAN EMPIRE, WHILE THE CULTURES OF THE THREE FORMER EMPIRES WERE STILL EXTANT. In confirmation, Jesus told his disciples in Luke 22:29: "And I appoint unto you a kingdom, as my father has appointed unto me." In other words he is relating to them that he was leaving to them, through his death, a kingdom. They were inheriting it, or it was being handed down to

The Descent of the Sons of God (A Parable)

them. He was placing them in a kingdom where they would be interacting and active. Judging from thrones, yet eating and drinking with him, or fellowshipping on the same level with him. It comes to my mind the question that Jesus asks John, "Can you drink of the same cup that I drink of?" Of course they answered "yes" and they did drink of that cup which was death. In his kingdom they would drink of the cup of eternal life, and he would share his table, as a Son with his Brethren, Sons of God, with equity.

Let's not forget the Apostle Paul writing in Galatians 1:15-16. "But when it pleased God, who separated me from my mother's womb, and called me by his grace, to reveal his son in me, that I might preach him among the heathen, immediately I conferred not with flesh and blood." "Reveal his son in me," means to uncover, as taking a lid off, or to uncover something hid. The words revealed "his son" really means he revealed "a Son" in me. Father unveiled the truth to Paul that within him was a SON of GOD. HE WAS A SON. He was placing him as a SON OF GOD. "LET'S TALK!" YOU CAN'T GET MORE SPIRITUAL THAN THIS or get more of a manifestation of the supernatural. You should be experiencing the supernatural daily. You should be experiencing him daily. You have the spirit of God in you and you have been placed as a son, who makes you a Son of God, which makes you super and natural, SUPERNATURAL.

The Ministering Angels

In April of 1998 my dad crossed over to the other side. A couple of weeks before his departure I had been invited to dinner and fellowship with a few friends. Evidently I ordered something that was spoiled and the consequences were apparent. Before I reached my home I was very ill and in intense pain. I changed my clothes quickly, thinking that if I could get into bed and be quiet, I would feel better. My pain didn't go away. In an hour I was so sick and nauseated I had to jump out of bed and run for the bathroom. I remembered praying as I sat on the floor shaking from the convulsive emptying of my stomach. I went back to bed again trying to get comfortable. Each time I would turn, the room would spin around and around. I finally lay in a fetal position rocking back and forth, thinking it would relieve the dizziness and keep my mind off of the pain. Thirty minutes passed and I was back in the bathroom again, repeating the violent spasmodic regurgitation. I was shaking so hard I had to hold onto the sink to support myself so I wouldn't fall. Tears began to stream down my face as the pain hit me again and I went to my knees. I clearly remember calling out, "Father, oh father, please help me!" I actually thought I was in the throes of death. Suddenly I felt two hands clasp my wrists, pulling me to my feet. I fell backward falling against what I thought was a wall, because it was so solid. I quickly turned my head to see who had hold of me. Through my tears I saw two angels, each had taken one of my wrists and stood me to my feet. I understood at that moment the wall I had fallen against was one of the angels. Wow, talk about Superman, the man of steel, he had nothing on them. Gently the angels took me into my bedroom and helped me into my bed as they placed their hands on my head ministering to me. Sometime during the early morning hours they helped me out of the bed, as I stood to my feet I took a step into another realm. I was

The Descent of the Sons of God (A Parable)

no longer in my room. I had stepped into the Spirit realm. I looked around me, people were everywhere. Some were lying down and some were sitting up. The angels were ministering to them. The atmosphere in that realm had a glorious aura of joy and that joy stayed with me for several months. When I came to myself, I was back in my room and in my bed, while the angels remained by my bedside in vigil.

When I awoke early the next morning, they were gone. I felt so much better, the moment my feet touched the floor, I felt the same glory I experienced in the Spirit realm. It was as if I walked and moved around in a glory cloud. I would sing to the Lord songs of praise in words that I remembered from the Psalms. I floated outside to my flower garden; I touched and talked to each plant. I leaned forward to walk under the branch of a tree that caused me to bend my head to look directly at the ground. I was laughing and singing as I moved under the tree branch and my eyes fell on four feet. Startled I put my hand to my mouth, as I let out a muffled scream. I raised my head, and looking up I saw the two angels, they were laughing at me. I began to laugh with them, and suddenly they were gone. Evidently they came to finish their assignment and went on their way. A few weeks later daddy went into the Spirit realm, before he left, I told him of my visitation. Daddy could not talk, yet his eyes lit up and with the biggest smile, he nodded in understanding. For months I walked in glory. I felt love, joy, and peace. I constantly hummed and sang to the Lord. I would say repeatedly, "Have I told you lately that I love you?" Nothing could penetrate that realm. I look back now and see how the Lord was preparing me for a crisis in my life that nearly made me buckle under the weight of the situation. The hardest thing for me was knowing I could not defend myself. I had to trust my father completely for the first time in my life. When I say completely I mean completely. I abandoned myself to him; it was all or nothing. I committed my life, spirit, soul and body to him. Then I sank my teeth into faith and trust as a dog with a new bone. I held on for life and that is exactly what happened, I held on for life, GOD LIFE.

As I experienced the glory, my prayer time became more passionate. Father began to reveal himself to me as well as myself to me. I didn't like myself, so I started running after him as the Shulamite in the Songs of Solomon, and he began to woo me. HEY! He has wooed me before, but not like this! Every time father would reveal a facet of himself to me I would be elevated into that glory realm and I would dance, sing, praise and weep daily; there would be weeks of pure glory. When it would lift I would face life as it is in the soulish realm. A month or so would pass and in my prayer time father would converse through my spirit, opening my understanding on different subjects in the word. I would receive it with joy, jumping joy, and I would jump right into that glory realm again. This has happened to the point that I am there more than I am in the soulish realm. Now you can understand how I could write this book; every chapter was interceded over. My father has prompted and coaxed me, giving me the words to write and to interpret the parable.

I want to go into more detail on the subject of "walking in the Spirit." Walking in the Spirit is not

The Descent of the Sons of God (A Parable)

something that happens overnight, or because you repetitiously confess the word, repetition can become ceremonial and become mere lip service. Being spiritual is not talking in the Spirit, or operating in the gifts of the spirit. Do you remember in the scriptures in Luke 14:28,29,30 where Jesus was teaching the multitudes, "For which of you, intending to build a tower, sitteth not down first, and counteth the cost, whether he have sufficient to finish it? Lest haply, after he hath laid the foundation, and is not able to finish it, all that behold it begin to mock him, saying this man began to build, and was not able to finish." I honestly believe, we who were in the old Pentecostal movement, started out moving and having our being in the spirit. Competition, pride, and ignorance brought us back to the soulish realm and we began to perform out of our soulish mind, and it became a religious ritual. Then we filed it under tradition and doctrine; that is exactly what it had become. "You do it this way or else," forget the many manifestations of the Spirit, if you were different it was heresy or wild fire. I wonder if Moses thought the burning bush was wild fire. His curiosity caused him to walk over to the bush and an angel begins to talk to him; there was a voice coming from the fire and it changed his life.

THE SCRIPTURE SAYS, FIRST YOU MUST BUILD A FOUNDATION! Children, we have a foundation the apostles laid for us, Jesus the cornerstone, the word, the foundation. We know this, yet the tower has to be built. You do not stop with just a foundation lying out there; that would mean you were a quitter. It is very sad to see a foundation of cement on a piece of ground never finished. Let's analyze this. If you want to build that tower, you must consider what the cost will be. Are you going to finish it? Are you committed? Can you pay the price? To truly walk in the Spirit is to commit. Paul said, "There is therefore now no condemnation to them which are in Christ Jesus, who walk not after the flesh, but after the Spirit." (Romans: 8:1) Do you realize the evidence of your walk in the Spirit is no condemnation and no damnation? You have to put your trust completely in father, you are a son and your past doesn't exist, you walk in the same realm with your father. Now the foundation is important and it is an integral part of the structure. The house or the tower or even the high rise gives us the message of a finished plan, an art that expresses "you." When you build on a spiritual foundation you are building a new house, whose expression is in another realm, where the real you is very apparent: not only in the spirit realm, but in the earthly realm also. Do you remember how you felt when you first confessed Jesus as Lord of you life and you realized you were a child of God and you immediately felt a bonding of love between you and your heavenly father? Unbeknown to you, your spirit was witnessing to you that God was your father. Your soul begins to call out, "ABBA FATHER, ABBA FATHER."

As a child of seven years old, spring had sprung. Everything was magnified to me. The grass sparkled from the rays of the sun, as if it had rained and the raindrops had turned to crystals. The songs of the birds that woke me early in the morning, the butterflies on my windowsill, the praying mantis: all of creation knew I was a Son of God and joined with me

The Descent of the Sons of God (A Parable)

in my celebration. I laughed a lot and really noticed friends and neighbors for the first time in my seven years, feeling a depth of love for them that I had not experienced before. I didn't focus on the bad around me, or the negative. I reveled in the ecstasy of joy. I felt such peace and love radiate from me and the presence of the spirit was everywhere. I would talk to my father as I jumped rope, hopscotched, played baseball or just walked home from school. I was a new person and everything everywhere was filled with the glory of God. I was experiencing the realm of the Spirit that was made accessible to me. I entered into the holy of holies, into the throne room and his scepter of righteousness was extended to me.

Walking in the Spirit is a life of progression, a progressive life and a climbing up, a life of ascent and descent. Understand this, when you descend, the glory that you dwell in, in your ascent, does not leave you, although, the earthly realm will veil your glory, it does not take it away. As you live and walk in the realm of the Spirit consistently, it will become a way of life. For instance, you will not judge or analyze, because you know how to control your thoughts. The one who controls all things is the judge. In this realm you see all people as the children of God, the body of Christ. Your thoughts are subject to your spirit. You learn to think like your spirit and you don't let your imagination get out of control by entertaining bad thoughts. You speak to your mind saying, I will not listen to you, and I will not hear negative thoughts about any one or anything. You rebuke them and ignore them; eventually you will see their dissipation. I am not saying they will not come, no, you will control them. I want to add this comment, when you walk in the Spirit, you do not ignore life and its vicissitudes. You see LIFE as it really is and you know how to respond as father would respond, because you have his nature, but you have to know his nature to walk in it. Father is just and compassionate and merciful: he is totally in control.

I thought I had finished this chapter but my spirit prompted me to write these words. John 10:33,34 and 35 reads: "The Jews answered him, saying, for a good work we stone thee not; but for blasphemy; and because that thou, being a man, makest thyself God. And Jesus answered them, it is not written in your law, I said ye are gods? If he called them gods, unto whom the word of God came, and the scriptures cannot be broken: say ye of him, whom the Father hath sanctified, and sent into the world, Thou blasphemest; because I said, I am the Son of God." Jesus said in 1st Timothy 4:7 "But refuse profane and old wives fables, and exercise thyself rather unto godliness." If you are really walking in the Spirit, you will know by the evidence and manifestations of the spirit in your life. Since Paul said to exercise yourself unto godliness, then it sounds to me that you have to practice being a god. To practice or to exercise unto godliness relates to me something that is done over and over and over, until you get it right. If yon know the nature of God, then act out the nature of GOD. Refuse to be unforgiving, unloving, critical, judgmental, selfish, depressed, angry, abusive and paranoid. I could go on and on giving to you the attributes of the flesh. Children, turn from this nature and walk in love, as God is love. To practice love is to practice godliness and it will be the solution to all the above.

The Descent of the Sons of God (A Parable)

Jesus spent many hours and many nights fellowshipping with father. You cannot know someone if you do not keep serious company with him. You will never know his nature or his voice if you never associate with him; his voice is his word. Listen to me, if you practice godliness, remember Jesus said, "Ye are gods and the scriptures cannot be divided or separated:" you can't take away from them, they are the same, today, yesterday and forever; then that tells me I must practice GOD-LIKE-NESS. I MUST START ACTING LIKE GOD! IF I START ACTING LIKE GOD, I sow to godliness. If I sow to godliness (God-like-ness), I will reap godliness (God like-ness). IN OTHER WORDS, I WILL REAP THE BENEFITS OF BEING A GOD! WOW! When you walk as God, you will reap as gods and you will live as gods!

The attributes of righteousness are holiness, innocence, justness and equity. This also is the nature of God and your nature, "the righteousness of God." The effects of his nature in you are peace, for in his eyes you are innocent, holy, just and equal. Equal to walk in the Spirit realm with him, having peace in doing so. This is what Paul meant, when he said, Jesus did not think it robbery, stealing or taking something away from God his father; to make himself equal with God. The many manifestations of God WERE seen in Jesus, because Jesus laid claim to, and took hold of that right as a son. He asserted his right as the SON OF GOD, AS THE SON OF A GOD, THEREFORE, REAPING THE BENEFITS OF A GOD, ALMIGHTY GOD. WHAT ARE THE BENEFITS? They are: eternal protection, eternal preservation, eternal healing, eternal deliverance, eternal provision and eternal peace of mind. What are

Marye Nicholas

the manifestations? The manifestations are: you being used as the Son of God to heal the nations, doing all the above. Father wants his Sons to assert their rights as Sons. Jesus WALKED ON WATER, healed the sick, raised the dead and fed the multitudes, which was the manifestation of his sowing and reaping unto Godliness and God-ness. The fruits of his works and the benefits of his works clearly bore evidence of he, Jesus, being a GOD!

The Descent of the Sons of God (A Parable)

Chapter 7

Romans 11:33 reads, "Oh the depth of the riches BOTH of the wisdom and knowledge of God! How unsearchable are his judgments and his ways past finding out!"

When I meditate on my spiritual origin, (believe me, I have spent hours with my father talking to him about it), I marvel at his wisdom and knowledge. The wisdom of God (Sophia in the Hebrew) looks from the end, to the beginning, where, man's wisdom looks at what is present, he doesn't consider the consequence of his actions, or entertain the end results. Man makes decisions on what he feels, or according to his senses. Father's decisions are made from the spirit, that which is of truth and righteousness.

When father began sending forth his word, to create all that we now see with the naked eye and all we cannot see in space, light years away: I have never once read where he made a mistake, or that he said, "WAIT, STOP, LET ME ERASE THAT, I WANT DO-OVERS!" No, the depth of his wisdom and knowledge is far beyond the capacity of human intelligence, whether it is through science, or technology, or any other intellectual phenomena, ALL, wisdom and knowledge comes from our father God.

Each generation father is releasing more of himself into the mind of man through man's spirit. Man's spirit is wisdom and knowledge, not his soul, his spirit. The spirit is the key to unlocking the door to the kingdom; opening to us POWER and AUTHORITY, RULING AND REIGNING. Jesus gave us these keys and we must learn to use them and activate them in our life until they become to us as natural as BREATHING. Eph. 4:4, 5 and 6 states, "There is one body and one spirit. One Lord, one father, one baptism, one God and father of all, who is above all and through all and in all." Man's spirit is God! THERE IS ONLY ONE SPIRIT AND THAT SPIRIT IS IN YOU! Children, I hope you realize that your spirit has the mind of God and is the mind of God. Your soul could never achieve anything without the spirit of God in you. Knowledge and wisdom is not "DROPPED" into your spirit, your spirit reveals it to your soul. You do not program your spirit; you renew your mind or your soul. You need to know the difference between your soul and your spirit and your renewed mind. Your renewed mind is the part of your mind that is learning the word and acting on it, that part of your mind we call spiritual mind. Your unrenewed mind is where your problem is: Wrong thinking, depression, hateful thoughts, unforgiveness, and confusion. Your mind can be controlled by taking authority over it and making it submit to the wisdom and knowledge of your spirit. Eventually you will learn what is soul and what is spirit, then you will start

The Descent of the Sons of God (A Parable)

walking in the depth of the riches of the wisdom and knowledge of God and his ways will be revealed to you.

I have made this a way of life for myself over the last three years. I have been astounded at how I have blossomed intellectually. I walk on a different level, higher than I have ever walked in my life. I love it! I laugh, I smile all the time, and I act silly when I want to act silly. I have a new personality. The inner expression of my father is being manifested outwardly and I am thrilled beyond words.

The eighth chapter of Proverbs explicitly defines wisdom. The following Hebrew translation is taken from the *Tanach, "Torah Prophets Writings."* Proverbs 8:12-35: "I am wisdom I dwell in cleverness; I provide knowledge of designs. Fear of Hashem (God) is hatred of evil. I hate pride and haughtiness, the way of evil, and a duplicitous mouth. With me there is counsel and wisdom; I am understanding; with me is might. Through me kings reign, and nobles will decree righteousness; through me officials will rule, and nobles, all who judge righteously. I love those who love me, and those who search for me shall find me. Wealth and honor are with me: great fortune and righteousness. My fruits are better than fine gold, even choice gold, and my produce is choicer than silver. I lead in the path of righteousness, amid the pathway of justice. I have substance to bequeath to those who love me, and I shall fill their storehouses. Hashem (God) made me as the beginning of his way, before his deeds of yore. I have reigned for all time: from the beginning, from before there was the earth. When there were no depths, I was formed; when there were no pools rich with water, before the mountains were

Marye Nicholas

settled, before the hills, I was formed: when He had not yet made the earth and its environs or the first dust of the inhabited world. When he prepared the heavens, I was there; when he etched out the globe upon the face of the depths; when he strengthened the heavens above; when he fortified the wellsprings of the depths; when he set for the sea its limit and the waters would not transgress His word; when he forged the foundations of the earth: I WAS THE NURSLING, I was his delight every day, playing before him at all times, playing in the inhabited areas of His earth, my delights are with the sons of man. And now children, listen to me; praiseworthy are those who heed to my ways. Harken unto discipline and grow wise and you will not reject wisdom. Praiseworthy is the person who listens to me, to hasten to my doors every day, to guard the doorposts of my entranceways. For one who finds me, finds life and elicits favor from Hashem (God), but one who sins against me despoils his soul; all who hate me love death." (end of translation)

Think about this, in the beginning, when everything, all creation was new, spoken forth by word from the mouth of father; that very word has nurtured creation for thousands of years. The word has nurtured it through progression, growth, expansion and multiplication, also division. It is the same with us, the Sons of God, his word spoke us forth, in fact, God was born in the earth, by his own word, the word made flesh. Father's word is spirit; his spirit is eternal. It stands to reason, we have been from eternity to eternity forever and everlasting. We are spirit and we have been, are and will always be nurtured by his word, by his spirit, because we are his substance, his Sons! One

The Descent of the Sons of God (A Parable)

more thing, I believe some things Father created, progresses in growth through time, producing the evidence of his spoken word, not every product of his creativity was instantaneous. His complete plan was made in wisdom and he had the knowledge to carry out every gigantic or minute detail. WE ARE THE PLAN! Philippians 3:20 reads, "For our conversation or citizenship has its fixed location in the heavens." We have a heavenly origin, a spiritual destiny. We are in the kingdom of God now! We have a responsibility to live a holy life on this earth. For the kingdom of God is in you! We must live a life that reflects the nature of our father, in the here and now! Not in the sweet bye and bye, but, ON THIS EARTH! We must discharge kingdom responsibility, as a citizen of his kingdom!

Marye Nicholas

The Descent of the Sons of God (A Parable)

Chapter 8

Psalms 19th chapter, a translation from the *Tanach Torah Prophets Writings*, page 1451: "The heavens declare the glory of God, and the firmament tells of his handiwork, day following day utters speech, and night following night declares knowledge. There is no speech and there are no words where their sound is not heard. Their precision goes forth throughout the earth, and their words reach the end of the inhabited world. In their midst he has set up a tent for the sun, which is like a groom emerging from his bridal chamber, it rejoices like a powerful warrior to run the course. Its source is the end of the heavens and its circuit is to their end and nothing is hidden, from its heat. The word of God is perfect, restoring the soul; the testimony of God is trustworthy, making the simple one wise; the orders of God are upright, gladdening the heart; the command of God is clear, enlightening the eyes; the fear of God is pure, enduring forever; the judgments of God are true, altogether righteous. They are more desirable than gold, than even much fine gold; and sweeter than honey, and dripping from the cones. Also when your servant is scrupulous in them, in observing them there is great reward. Who can discern mistakes? Cleanse me from unperceived faults. Also from intentional sins restrain your servant; let them not rule me, then I shall be perfect; and I will be cleansed of great transgression. May the expressions of my mouth and the thoughts of my heart find favor before you, God my Rock and my Redeemer."

David is awed by the beauty, splendor and glory of the handiwork of God in the heavens. He is overwhelmed by the fact that there is not a word spoken or a sound declaring, "look at us, look what God did!" The beauty of God's creation speaks for itself, to the ends of the earth. You can see his glory forever and ever in a sky that never ends. The knowledge of God is seen in the universes, galaxies, gravitational fields, rotation of the earth, in the sun, stars and planets, all remain in orbit, positioned by his word; in their silence they declare the majesty of God. There is one thing that bothers David as he looks into the heavens. Everything is perfect, yet something is lacking in perfection; that something is man. David realizes that he is in that category and desires to break away from the enslavement of his human nature and offenses. He wants to be perfect and sinless, functioning in the order and plan that God has ordained for him; he wants to fulfill his destiny in the earth. David declares God's word and judgments are pure and righteous and will restore and cleanse the soul of man, as it was in the beginning. In summation David is saying that the heavens can't declare in words or sounds the glory of God, but I can. I will express the

The Descent of the Sons of God (A Parable)

thoughts of my heart, in words from my mouth, of your magnificence, oh God my Redeemer.

There are days and nights in my own life that I marvel at the works of my father's hands. It astounds me to know that the stars are now giving us a glimpse of the early universe. We are able now, thanks to astronomy, to look at objects a billion light years away. In fact, we are really looking a billion years back into time, because it took a billion years for the light from some stars to reach us. When we look at a star we don't see it as it is now, but as it was when the light left its surface in the beginning.

Why are stars fascinating to me? Stars are fascinating to me because I was in my father the Ancient of Days, when the first stars were created by his knowledge and wisdom, then spoken forth by the word of his mouth. As the light of the stars created in the beginning come closer to the earth, one can see with the naked eye the wonders of the evidence of an infant, pure earth that existed in the beginning, and the evidence of our eternal existence with him and in him, as Sons of God.

I read in a commentary from the *TALMUDIC MIDRASHIC AND RABBBINIC SOURCES*, a comment made by some of the rabbis about Adam and David. In agreement they arrived at the conclusion that Adam was the first Son of God chosen to keep all creation in harmony. God had positioned every heavenly body, heavenly hosts, oceans, trees, land, beast, fish, cattle and fowls in the heavens and earth to perform in harmony as in a great symphony. As long as all creation was in harmony, there would be peace and there would be one voice. Adam's position in the universe was to be the conductor. As he conducted the voices of praise, he received the melody of praise as the creator, instead of the conductor. Figuratively speaking his baton was taken away and he lost his position as one that kept harmony. When David was born his destiny was not only to be a king; but he was chosen to take his place as the conductor. He would bring back the harmony through his songs, or Psalms he composed and the instruments he made: he would bring harmony once again to the heavens and earth through beautiful melodies and praise.

David specifically brings out this point in the eighth Psalm when he says, "Who is man that you are mindful of him?" or that your mind is full of him and you even visit him; you have encircled him by crowning him with your glory. Remember God's glory is his spirit. Let's say it like this, you have fenced him in with flesh and bone and then you put yourself within him by crowning him with the glory of your spirit. Think about it, here is man clothed in the heavens and the earth. The sun, moon and stars UNDER HIS FEET, all creation handed to him by his father God to rule over. All things were subject or a servant to him. Another oops, Adam failed but Jesus didn't! We are brought back again into harmony with God through the LORD JESUS CHRIST. We must join with all creation lifting our voices as one voice in praise daily, exalting his name, as he conducts all creatures and all creation into a melodious song of praise, magnifying him as our creator.

In the parable I talked about father taking his sons into the universe to create with their spoken word. For years we have been taught that our words of faith

The Descent of the Sons of God (A Parable)

are creative; the negative can be as creative as the positive. In fact, we put more emphases on the negative because we are not aware of our negativism. It is easier to speak out of hatred or anger, or just a plain bad attitude, than it is to build yourself up in faith through the word. You don't have to build yourself up to be negative, because man's nature is to be negative; either way negative or positive, your words are creative. I must admit I have been dealt with about my words and I believe I have learned the lesson well. I HAVE LEARNED TO STOP MY BAD THOUGHTS WHEN THEY COME. I cringe when I hear bad reports on people, reports that never change. For instance, I have heard ministries dam God's people, spewing out judgment and words of wrath. I have heard people repeat stories with a "they will never change" attitude. I have seen people who find something wrong with everyone they meet, if it isn't their features it is their anatomy or their personality. I have heard words spoken over drug addicts, habitual smokers and alcoholics saying, "that person will never change, or they will die in their filth, sinners that will split hell wide open, having no hope."

Our words are powerful! It may be your words that have set the course of no hope for that husband, child or wife. In reality you are actually covenanting with death over that person. You are planting words in the earth that will spring up in their time and season setting the course of their direction into depravation and ruin. As a seed planted takes time and nurturing to come out of the ground strong and productive, so also the words that you sow over people repeatedly, will continue to produce.

Marye Nicholas

Bad confessions can be in any area of your life: financial, health and business. My son and his wife never say, "We can't afford it!" They say, "It isn't in our budget at this moment." Change your thought line and your words. Let Grace come forth from your mouth; words that bless and that will turn the course of a man, woman and child's life. Remember the old saying, "Rome wasn't built in a day." Brand that into your mind, not your spirit, for your spirit already knows the things of the Spirit. Reverse your negative THOUGHTS AND WORDS. Let your positive good words constantly nurture the good seed you've planted; bless, bless, and bless.

One of the most important lessons you will have to learn in life is to trust the Spirit of your father. That same spirit is in you, teaching you all things. Trust him in every situation. He is in control and your footsteps are ordained. Trust the Spirit of your father that is in the world, as he is in control, he reconciled the world unto himself. It was a done deal. That same Spirit is working eternally and does not cease, ever! He is reconciling and restoring that we might be saved to the uttermost. He will go to any length to create a way to change a situation or circumstance.

Now since God is in control and he is omnipresent, then you have to trust his Spirit in your son, daughter, loved one, husband or wife. When you learn to rest in this, time means nothing to you. Trust has no time limit. I saw it happen in my daughter. I stopped the negative words and agreed with my spirit for her deliverance. I rejoiced in that day years before it came. Praise God she is a blessing, she was lost to me once, but now she is found. Learn to speak

The Descent of the Sons of God (A Parable)

nurturing words over and over, then you will set the course of nature in the right direction. When you get serious and set your mind to trust God, you will start seeing a change in your outlook on life.

Since I have changed my words and thoughts, I see things differently, and I see the world differently. I feel a love for people I never felt before in such intensity. I see the face of God all around me and I feel his presence to the point of total awareness. Remember the Shulamite in the Songs Of Solomon? Solomon was sitting at his table, while Abishag was hoping he would notice her by the scent of her fragrance that permeated the room where he sat. The presence of that fragrance gave out a clear message, "Abishag, your beloved is near!" The presence of the fragrance of our beloved creates an environment of joyfulness, love, newness, laughter and a merry heart. We feel the electricity or vibes, as some would call it, everywhere we go. You totally forget yourself and somehow emerge into that love, because the thoughts of your mind are focused on him. You begin to function according to the measure of the glory you perceive of him and the more perception and interaction with him, the greater he will be expressed in you, his BELOVED!

My BELOVED is eternal. I saw him among the universes when the earth was newly born, created in the beginning, billions of years ago. I see him now, in the universe, which has become mature as he himself; the ANCIENT OF DAYS. Galaxies, quasars, spirals and clusters of stars, whose light we are now seeing with the naked eye; created in the beginning light years away. I see the face of MY BELOVED in their light as it moves toward us bringing us evidence of universes and worlds that have expanded into many worlds and universes: worlds of moons, planets and stars. I see the face of MY BELOVED beyond the firmament, beyond the ability of man's eye to see; north, south, east and west hemispheres, with stars as numerous as gold dust, appearing as glittering paved diamonds in the heavens. I see the face of MY BELOVED in the oceans with their boisterous sounds, as their waves dash against the shores. I hear his laughter and voice in the quiet trickling of the brooks, streams and springs as the water plays among the rocks and pebbles. I see the face of MY BELOVED in the clouds with all of their forms and images, as they move across the sky, oh so white against a background of blue. I see the face of MY BELOVED in the sun, whose glory is in its brightness, for its brightness is the light of the world. I see him in the mountains, hills, and valleys, with plush terrains of trees and foliage as far as the eye can see. Beasts of the fields, cattle, sheep and fowl of the air, large and small, in the beautiful face of a fawn to the intricate delicate colors of a tiny beta fish, whose world is in a sculptured crystal vase. I see the face of MY BELOVED in all of creation, as he embraces the universes and worlds with the fragrance of his presence. He is the universe and all it contains. All things evolve in him and around him.

Daily you can see the face of MY BELOVED expressed in his children, in a father, mother, son and daughter, from infancy to maturity, from death to life, made in his image in an eternity that is unending. Draw me to you oh my beloved and I will run after you. When you take us into your chambers we will rejoice and be glad.

The Descent of the Sons of God (A Parable)

Chapter 9

St. John 14:12, "In my father's house are many mansions, rooms and dwelling places. If it were not true, if it were not a reality, I would have told you so. I go to prepare, make ready or create a place for you; and when I come again I will receive, or take you unto myself, that where I am you may be also." I go to "prepare" means to thoroughly make ready. It also speaks of internal fitness, referring to the spirit. I am going to the cross, grave and then to my father; so you can once again, be quickened in the spirit and made alive. You will become my dwelling place, a room for the Godhead, a temple for my glory.

1st Kings the sixth chapter tells the story of King Solomon. Solomon, according to the pattern, built a beautiful Temple, the first Temple. In that Temple were many rooms that were arranged in successive stories against the sanctuary, where the priest would stay during their course of service. Over the Most Holy Place Solomon built two chambers overlaid in gold, accessible only to the kings and high priests: 2nd Chronicles 3:8-9. King Herod's Temple was much larger and extravagantly beautiful, also having many rooms, chambers and dwelling places. There is an earthly temple and there is a spiritual Temple. We are the spiritual Temple. We are the rooms and UPPER chambers OVER LAID IN GOLD in the Father's House. We are being made ready, prepared as dwelling places individually and corporeally for the Glory of God. Each room is filled with glory, expressing WHOLLY the fullness of the Godhead and SHEKINAH GLORY. Solomon's temple was an earthly temple. Children, we will not be limited to the earthly, we are the Temple of the living God and will be prepared and made ready to contain his glory.

The holy vessels, candlesticks, bread, light, alter, alter of incense, brazen sea, laver, the Holy Place and the Most Holy Place were symbols of Jesus; a pattern of things to come. Jesus went back into the father once again, to take his place as King of Kings and Lord of Lords. He had kept his brethren and manifested the name of his father unto the men, his disciples that his father had given to him; he had kept them, in his name. Jesus was the pattern son and the pattern God. He made evident the nature of his father and expressed that nature as a son. Every name, covenant name, functioned in Jesus and was manifested in him and through him, so, when Jesus ascended to take up where he left off before coming to the earth, he left us a pattern. We became and are functioning as the vessels, the light, the bread, incense, Holy Place and the Most Holy Place, plus, every name of God is manifested through us and in us. In other words his whole identity and nature and all that he is, is alive in our whole being. When you have a pattern you do not cut the pattern to the material, you

The Descent of the Sons of God (A Parable)

cut the material to the pattern; after the garment is made you have an original. You were cut from the pattern Son; he went on to reign as Almighty GOD; THE PATTERN BECAME THE ORIGINAL GOD. Now, YOU have been cut, formed and shaped from the pattern of the Son of God. You have taken his place as the Son. YOU, now are the ORIGINAL, you are the SON! Jesus fulfilled his destiny and purpose and looks on us as the finished product, so since you are a finished product, there are no more patterns to pass on or fulfill. Children, WE ARE IT, THERE ARE NO MORE SYMBOLS OR PATTERNS. WE HAVE FULFILLED OUR DESTINY AND PURPOSE, TAKING OUR PLACE AS THE SON OF RIGHTEOUSNESS.

Marye Nicholas

The Descent of the Sons of God (A Parable)

Chapter 10

Matthew 5:14 reads, "Ye are the light of the world. A city that is set on a hill cannot be hid." Jesus was calling the people "A city." I just answered a question I asked myself. Israel was the only nation that worshiped a living God. He wanted to exalt his people and make them an example. He wanted to set them on high so they couldn't be hid, an example and a light to all nations, and for all nations to see.

There were five mountains that the city was built on: Mt. Moriah (chosen by Jehovah) Acra, Bezetha, Ophel, and Mt. Zion.

Many Jewish commentaries perceive an allusion to the dual existence of Jerusalem. A heavenly Jerusalem and an earthly Jerusalem, representing a utopian ideal of a perfect city, totally in harmony with God's wishes. When David designed earthly Jerusalem he modeled it upon the example of heavenly Jerusalem and made every effort that both cities should become like a city that is united together.

Marye Nicholas

The rabbis have an arrogant attitude about the origin of the name or Jerusalem, which is commonly known as "the foundation, the dwelling place, the habitation of peace or the inheritance of peace." They believe the name was comprised of Jireh and Shalem. Abraham called it Jehovah-Jireh, while Shem called it Shalem. God in all his infinite wisdom put the two names together and named it Jireh-Shalem, Jerushalaim, or Jerusalem. The city was a joy to all of its inhabitants and a festive city that was engraved in the palm of his hand: a pattern of the heavenly city.

I will never forget the first time I read of the destruction of the temple and the city of Jerusalem. The stately walled city, seemingly indestructible, was captured and destroyed by Titus of Rome.

In 70 A.D. as Jesus predicted, not one stone remained upon another. Thousands had been incinerated, murdered, starved to death and yes, crucified outside the walls.

I copied this article from the book "*SAND AND STARS*" the Jewish journey through time: written by Yaffa Ganz. "Rome's greatest bitterest war was over, Titus had captured 100,000 prisoners, countless thousands had been killed, thousands were sold as slaves and thousands were forced to fight wild animals in the Roman coliseums to entertain the bloodthirsty mobs.

Titus had cut down every tree within twenty miles of Jerusalem: centuries old olive trees, cedars, vineyards and fruit trees. Judea the "BRIGHTEST JEWEL ON EARTH" was now desolate and now smoking bare.

The Descent of the Sons of God (A Parable)

Titus took vast wealth from the temple treasury, taking hordes of gold and silver vessels. He took seven hundred of the handsomest young Jewish men to Italy to march in an impressive victory parade through the jeering crowds, in the streets of Rome. Titus built a towering stone gate, "the Arch of Titus" in honor of his victory. And he minted victory coins with the words "Judea Capta" – Judea is captive."

For two thousands years, ever since the destruction of the second temple, the Jewish people have been scattered across the face of the earth, yet they remain loyal to God and loyal to his word.

Children, there is hope! Praise the Lord! You are the NEW JERUSALEM, indestructible, high and lifted up, elevated to glorious heights, coming from the realm of the Spirit, coming from GOD. YOU ARE THE CITY THAT IS THE LIGHT OF THE WORLD, a city that can't be shaken. The river of life that runs through the city makes glad your heart.

A city can't be a city unless it has people. It can have high rises, office buildings, houses, highways, streets, parks and churches but, without people you have empty places and empty rooms. The people make the city, YOU ARE THE CITY!

And the foundation of the wall of that city, were garnished with all manner of precious stones; lively stones, tried, tested, formed and shaped in the earth, prepared for the New Jerusalem, a city not made with hands. We are jewels that make one lustrous stone set solidly, mounted in pure gold, mounted and set solidly in God (deity), coming down from God, or coming out of God as a bride made ready for her husband. Eve was taken from Adam; molded, shaped and given life. We were molded, shaped and formed in father; we will come forth from him as one who has always been with him, eternal and perfect.

I read in the *Tehillim* (Psalms) a commentary from Talmudic, Midrashic and Rabbinic sources an interesting thought. The woman is the glory of the man, and the Shekinah Glory in Jerusalem is spoken of in the feminine and is as a bride, the Shekinah Glory of her husband. We are the city and the bride and the precious jewels that adorn the walls as the ornaments of a bride. The word tells us in the 46th Psalm that praise is comely for the saints. Let me phrase it like this, praise is as an ornament and makes you beautiful to your Lord. So shall the king greatly desire thy beauty, for he is your Lord, worship thou him. The King's daughter is all glorious within; her clothing is of wrought gold. She has clothed herself in God and has put on her priestly garments, and will make his name to be remembered in all generations; therefore shall the people praise you forever, for out of Jerusalem the perfection of beauty is shining.

Tanach Torah Prophet Writings page 1041, Isaiah 49:14 interprets this passage of scripture beautifully. Zion said; "God has forsaken me, my lord has forgotten me. Can a woman forget her baby, or not feel compassion for the child of her womb? Even these may forget, but I will not forget you. Behold I have engraved you on my palms; your walls are before me always. Your children will hasten to return and your ruiners and destroyers will leave you. Raise your eyes all around to see. They have gathered, they will come to you. As I live, the word of God I swear, that you will clothe yourself with them all like jewelry and

The Descent of the Sons of God (A Parable)

adorn yourself like a bride." Jerusalem will clothe herself with her sons and daughters and wear them like jewels as a bride adorned with her bridal ornaments prepared and made beautiful for her husband.

Here is a thought you might meditate on. Since there is nothing new to be introduced and we are the original and only Sons of God, what is before us? We would be naive to think, "This is it!" There are worlds in the heavens and in the realm of the spirit we know nothing about, because our finite mind can't remember its origin. Is there something in another world, another dimension of the Spirit, in the future, somewhere, where, we may be the PATTERN SONS, PATTERN gods TO A NEW CREATION?

Marye Nicholas

The Descent of the Sons of God (A Parable)

Revealing Of A Son

Chapter 11

On November the sixteenth 1966, my son Jonathan Nicholas made his entrance into this earthly realm we call " The world." Because of my history of long labor, my doctor decided he would take matters into his own hands and hurry things along. During the delivery, my spirit left my body and I entered the spirit realm.

I entered into a garden, the same garden that Adam and Eve walked in, east of Eden. I looked around at the eternal beauty of the fragrant flowers and trees with foliage of deep rich colors. Life was vibrant and dazzling, from a blade of grass to the dewdrops that seemed to cling to the petals and leaves of the trees and flowers. It didn't surprise me to see many people in the garden realm, but it was more surprising to see the deep concern expressed on their faces; the concern was for my son and myself.

I heard a voice; it was the voice of my father as he walked through the garden. What amazed me most of all was that I, at times, was very aware of my physical condition, yet at other times I was totally unaware because I was not pregnant in the spirit realm. At times I must have hovered momentarily between the boundaries of the soul and the spirit; the earth does have a pull upon the soul.

When I heard my father's voice I became oblivious to the many people about me. It was as if my father overshadowed me. His presence became as a pavilion around about me, comforting me, while explaining to me the birth of a son. How appropriate for my father who planned his family and their destiny to share with me his plan. The soft tone of his voice drew me to him, into a presence of love that is indescribable. It was as if he and I were the only two beings in his garden realm. He began to speak.

"From the beginning I have had a plan to create male and female to inhabit the earth. I would place them in this garden and would walk and talk with them and teach them everything that would be necessary for them to rule the earth. I created them to reproduce, to have children and become families filling the earth. Sons and daughters would be born inheriting the characteristics of their parents, talents and gifts handed down through the generational bloodline. Each generation would function in their inheritance, gifts and talents, taking them to a higher level." I meditate on his words and think, what a father! If the children take their intellect, gifts and talents to another level then each generation would be teaching the generation before them and after them. Talk about ruling as SONS OF GOD! EVERYONE WOULD LEARN FROM EACH OTHER, having all

The Descent of the Sons of God (A Parable)

knowledge and all authority. NO BIG I, AND NO LITTLE YOU.

My father told me that I would have a son and that he would inherit my talents, gifts and characteristics. He continued on saying, "You will raise this child and direct his way by teaching him of me and my word." I remember during our conversation I heard the voices of the doctors and nurses as they worked in the delivery room. I would go back into the spirit realm and father would comfort me.

Finally he turned to me and told me it was time to go. I left to come back into his presence, meeting him in a different place. Father met me at an area between earth and the spirit realm. I asked him to let me come into that realm, actually we did not speak with our voices, we talked thought to thought, mind to mind. In this place was darkness; I saw his form, not with my eyes, but in my mind. We stood in a place that seemed to be a boundary separating the spirit from the earthly. I asked father to let me come back and he answered, "No you can't stay, you have to go back, you have to raise your son." I came back into his presence approximately three times and was denied entrance. He was very compassionate and loving and his peace filled the place where we met, yet he was firm in his decision.

When I awoke I was in the recovery room. However, the nurses thought I was still out from the anesthetic and so they talked of Jonathan's delivery and how close we came to death. A decision was made in the realm of decision, I had a commission and I would fill it.

Marye Nicholas

My son was born at 2:00 a.m. Franklin, my husband, came into my room with Jonathan in his arms; what I am about to say I have never shared with anyone except my heavenly father. Franklin leaned down to hold Jonathan in a position so that I could see him eye to eye as he said, "Here is your son; son here is your mother." I saw a beautiful little face, a perfect baby wrapped tightly in a birthing blanket, weighing in at 8 lbs. and 13 oz. Jonathan's eyes turned towards me; as our eyes met I didn't look into the eyes of an infant, I looked into the eyes of my father in all of his maturity, intellect and wisdom: "The Ancient Of Days." Thereby confirming the conversation we shared in the garden realm.

If Mary the mother of Jesus had only known what I knew, she would have seen the Master, the Eternal Father, The Great EL-ELYONE in the eyes of baby Jesus. This is why I know I am of his substance. One day my soul will be of the same nature of my spirit, and one with my spirit, which is his spirit, knowing all things.

The Revealing of the Son.

When Franklin said, "Here is your son; son here is your mother," it was the time of "the revealing of a child." From that day forth, November 16th 1966, Jonathan's nature, his soulish nature, would develop. I won't dwell on mischievous ways and disruptive boyish pranks; being an only boy with three older sisters, one could expect chaos at times. I never saw the side of him that my daughters and relatives talk about. I saw an innocent little boy, "my baby!" I watched him for twenty years observing his nature. I saw the characteristics and mannerism of his dad in

The Descent of the Sons of God (A Parable)

him, yet my own characteristics were predominate in many ways. Despite the onset of the unpredictable teenage years and the devastation it can bring to a parent, it was not so with Jonathan. He was a very special child and soared through them unscathed by the world system.

A Revealing of the Spirit:

Jonathan made a decision early in his life. He made a choice. Deuteronomy the eleventh chapter is filled with promises to those that choose good over evil; it is a choice that becomes a way of life. It is a transition from one realm to another, from the earthly to the spiritual. Several years passed into his adult life as he adjusted to the protocol of the spirit. I saw a new nature coming forth, pushing through that soulish man and expressing his real identity; the identity that comes from the substance of God, that he took from himself, that nature that has been handed down to us, million of years ago; an inheritance of all that our father is and ever will be!

GOD'S NATURE IS THE ENTRANCE OF THE WORD to our mind. (Psalms119:130) So many times I have heard people say, I know the word in my mind now I need to get it in my spirit. No you need to get it in your mind, your mind is what is renewed. If this tabernacle were dissolved you would see that your spirit knows all things. It could quote the word from Genesis to Revelations. "For you have the mind of Christ." (1st Corinthians. 2:16) Where do you have the mind of Christ? Your spirit has the mind of Christ. Your mind receives the mind of Christ through the word.

Marye Nicholas

I see the expression of my father in my son. I see the nature of God in him as a Son of God. I am not the only one to see Jesus, whom is the nature of God, but also his congregation, his children, his business associates and his wife see that nature. How does one see the nature of our father in his children? First of all, in a moment-by-moment walk. I see it in my son when he sings. He has one of the most beautiful baritone voices you will ever hear in your lifetime. Since he is en-christed, he never has to ask for the anointing, it comes along with the territory. He has a photographic memory and this gift has enabled him to excel in his position as a businessman and as a pastor teaching the word. If I am aware of this nature, the expression of it and the evidence of it, then my Son is being revealed to me as a Son of God, therefore, GOD IS BEING REVEALED TO US.

In one of the previous chapters I mentioned the scripture Jesus waxed strong in spirit. (Luke 2:40) The reason for the waxing strong in spirit was that the soul at a young age began to decrease, and the spirit increased. John the Baptist said, "I must decrease and he must increase." John represented that which was earthy. Jesus represented that which was spirit. Jesus was revealed as a man, as a Son, not as a GOD to mankind. Israel and all of his kin received the revealing of a man; later the disciple's eyes were opened to the revelation that he was the Son of God. But Israel did not know God. The only God they knew of was carried around in an Ark. Jesus couldn't be God, he wasn't a king, he wasn't wealthy and he didn't have an army with thousands of warriors. "It wasn't

The Descent of the Sons of God (A Parable)

God doing all of the miracles, it was a prophet." How utterly sad, that God himself walked among them.

(Psalms 81:13) "Oh that my people had hearkened unto me and Israel had walked in my ways! I should have soon subdued their enemies, and turned my hands against their adversaries. The haters of the Lord should have submitted themselves unto him: but their time, Israel's time, should have endured FOREVER. He should have fed them also with the finest of the wheat: and with honey out of the rock should I have satisfied thee." What a promise to us who are under the new covenant. His ways are his nature; if you walk in his nature he will subdue our enemies and we would live and endure forever. He would feed us the finest of wheat (bread, word) and with honey out of the rock he would satisfy us spiritually and physically. The Rock is Jesus: honey comes forth from our Rock. Whew! Pour forth that Honey on me father, I receive the pouring forth in every area of my life.

Meditate on this… honey is possibly the sweetest substance that one will taste. Imagine honey being poured all over you, think spiritually; you are becoming one with the sweetest, purest honey. Honey is symbolically the nature of God; pure and sweet, nothing can compare to that sweet pure nature. Let me say it like this, with the GOD nature that comes from Jesus the Rock, I will satisfy you and that nature will make you complete.

Marye Nicholas

The Descent of the Sons of God (A Parable)

: Revealing of Sons in High Places. Ephesians 2:6 "And hath raised us up together and made us sit together in heavenly places in Christ Jesus."

Chapter 12

At a very young age father begin to reveal himself as "father" to Jesus. We see this throughout his life and in his conversations to the Sadducees and Pharisees. To hear Jesus a mere man, maybe a prophet, most assuredly an insurrectionist, call God his father? Never! That was unthinkable; it was a sin and sacrilege. By the time Jesus began his ministry, he knew his father intimately, since he knew God as his father, it stands to reason he knew he was a son, God's Son. It was normal and very natural to say, "My father is with me I am not alone. My father and I are one, or, my father loves me and before Abraham I AM." The revelation was being revealed to him that he was a Son and last of all, but not least, he was ALMIGHTY GOD.

Everything about Jesus manifested the character and nature of Father God; his portraying of his father's word, his walk, his prayer life, all came from absolute trust and emersion of himself into his father. All the above was a way of life for the Son of God, our brother, especially his prayer life. Evidently it was not sporadic, as the majority of the people's prayer lives are in the world today. As I said it was a way of life, and it *was* life manifesting through him. He also was visited and ministered to by angels and knew the voice of his father, as the fullness of the God Head functioned in him with all power. This is why he was convinced of who he was.

I mentioned in a previous chapter that Jesus gave evidence of his deity through healing, miracles and authority over the elements, which included walking on the water. Could you honestly say you believe in your father and trust him as a Son, to the point of stepping into the ocean, and walking on the water as if it were dry ground? I haven't read any headlines lately of water-walkers, or hurricane stoppers. I haven't read any headlines saying, that "Sons of God have risen and are taking their places in the earth, raised in heavenly places, high places in the earth functioning in power and might, as GOD himself" Children we need to get the revelation of our origin and who we are. We are father's family, his SONS AND DAUGHTERS.

After spending ALL night in prayer Jesus proceeded to choose his disciples. His disciples had been revealed to him as his disciples and as his brethren. He knew that his father had given them to him for they were the father's from the beginning. He was to tell them of their future and their destiny. They were sent here for the purpose of continuing his

The Descent of the Sons of God (A Parable)

ministry OF LIFE as the Corporate Son in the earth. John 15:16-19 proclaims, "Ye have not chosen me but I have chosen you and ordained you that you should go forth and bare fruit, and that your fruit should remain. Ye are not of this world, but I have chosen you out of the world therefore the world hates you."

On the other hand little by little and step by step Jesus was being revealed to his disciples. Luke 16:29-30, "His disciples said unto him: so now speakest thou plainly and speakest no proverb. Now we are sure you knowest all things, and needest not that any man should ask thee: but this we believe that thou camest forth from God." It was after the resurrection that the disciples really begin to understand the revelation. The depth of the revelation came after Paul's conversion. He revealed Jesus as God the Father, as king of Kings and Lord of Lords. The revelation, "being in him before the foundations of the earth," should have blown their minds. Remember what Peter said about Paul, "Some of the things he said were hard to understand." (Paraphrase) Paul specifically states that we are Sons of God, A CORPORATE BODY, A FAMILY, RAISED OUT OF DARKNESS and PLACED BACK INTO OUR FATHER IN CHRIST JESUS.

The heavenly places as I have so adamantly declared is our receiving the revelation of our son-ship accepting the truth that we received Jesus' glory and he received the Father's glory. He returned to a position he had before the world was created. God the father, God the creator; we walk into our inheritance, which is the position of the Son, functioning in every capacity; in the glory he gave us.

Marye Nicholas

When you get finished with this book I pray you will know father as a real father. I want you to see the love he has for his children. I want you to know your origin before your earthly birth and that there was a plan for mankind to come to a state of eternal perfection. It would take time for the soul of man to reach that state. That is why I say, " <u>before the cross the revealing of the soul, after the cross the revealing of the spirit.</u>"

I want to give you one more example of the revealing of a son in high places. I must admit the disciples in their walk with the Lord never envisioned him as king or the creator, because they knew him as a man first. Had he come into Jerusalem in wealth and glory, there is a possibility that all would have accepted him.

I am very intrigued with the story of Joseph whose life was so much like our Lords. Symbolically we see Jesus in Joseph, a type of Christ. The story in Genesis relates to us a child that was loved dearly by his father and he was the apple of his father's eye. Joseph wore a coat of many colors, the evidence of his birthright, in other words he was clothed in his birthright. <u>We as sons are clothed in ours</u> that Jesus passed on to us, an <u>inheritance that guarantees our rights as sons.</u> Joseph's brothers would cringe each time they saw Joseph with his coat on. It was like a neon light flashing: "birthright, birthright." It was a constant reminder of the favoritism of their father toward Joseph. "The audacity of this younger brother to tell them his pompous dreams of grandeur: they would bow down to him, yeah right!" I can imagine the thoughts of the brothers as they saw Joseph in the

The Descent of the Sons of God (A Parable)

distance, walking in the fields toward them. "Here comes the spy, little motor mouth, daddies baby, let's get rid of him!" Their jealousy and envy prompted them to consider taking his life; not realizing that their actions were responding to a plan of God for their future redemption. They sold Joseph to a band of Ishmaelite, and they sold him as a slave in Egypt, but not without stripping him of his coat that signified his birthright, killed a kid and dipped that coat in the blood of that kid. Unbeknown to the brothers that kid's blood that was applied to that coat covered Joseph life, a symbol and type of the blood of Jesus. The son was giving his life that his brethren would live. Another promise was being set in order. God had told Abraham his seed would go into Egypt, adding that the seed would also come out. Joseph was being placed as a son, to be revealed in Egypt, and later he would be revealed to his brethren, as a Son, a Brother, Redeemer and a King.

Before the revealing of a son there is testing. A son has to be formed and molded and shaped to bring out the real nature that is in him, the real you, you the spirit.

Evidently Joseph got the revelation of "THE PLAN." When he accessed his life and dreams, he knew something far more glorious, was being initiated for his future. He put himself in the plan under the hand of God, trusting him completely, which eventually raised him, into heavenly places.

How pathetic the scene when Joseph's brothers arrived in Egypt. Only a beloved brother would recognize his family camouflaged by the dust and dirt of along tedious journey. The brothers did not recognize

Marye Nicholas

Joseph because of his Egyptian attire and because he was a king. When he walked in his domain or rode in his chariot the servants called out before him, AVREC, which is a composition of two words: 'Av'- father, mentor and counselor, the last four letter 'rech' or 'rach' means king in the Aramaic. It never entered their minds that they would ever see their brother again much less consider his dreams as becoming a reality. In all of their imaginings they never entertained the thought that their brother was a king and their lives would be in his hands.

Joseph placed his brothers at a table in the order of their birth, which astonished them to no end. This was a clue to his revealing and they couldn't comprehend it. After severe testing of his brothers, he saw them come to the defense of Benjamin; they had changed. Then, JOSEPH REVEALS HIMSELF TO HIS BRETHREN; that's when they saw the family resemblance. "I in you and you in me, also we are one, for we come from our father." How precious the revealing when it comes: the weeping, the humbling, the acknowledging and the sharing of the revelation.

In Egypt, Israel's family was kept in the name of the one who had the birthright. To say the name of Joseph would mean nothing to the Egyptians, but to say the name Zaphnath-paaneah (he who reveals that which is hidden) every knee bowed. Joseph was the type of Christ, Benjamin the type of us, the younger son, whom receives the greater portion. We are the son of his right hand, "greater things shall we do, because he went back, to the father."

John 17:6-11, I have manifested your name unto them and I have kept them in the name you gave

The Descent of the Sons of God (A Parable)

me. Holy Father, keep through thine own name those, whom you have given me.

I understand the <u>name</u> is one's identity and that this particular scripture may refer to the covenant names of God and all of the natures or personalities of those names. However, somehow I see it in a different way. Jesus explicitly and boldly declares his love for his father and his father's love for him. Father means: head of a family, parent and protector. Could it be that he was introducing the word father, instead of God, to his family, since father was the loving head of his family? "Let them know, you love them, as you love me. I have kept guarded and protected them by the father identity, nature and love you have given me." That father nature and identity functioned in Jesus because he and the father were one, he saturated them (the disciples) with it and he baptized them in it. He was expressing a new thing, an agape love that was foreign to man. That name and nature he was keeping them in, and enfolding and wrapping them in, was their father, and they were his sons. Jesus was revealing the Father to his family, the Sons of God.

Marye Nicholas

The Descent of the Sons of God (A Parable)

Chapter 13: The Sealing Of The Sons.

Jeremiah 32:8-12 *Tanach Torah Prophet Writings*, page 1147.

"My cousin Hanamel came to me, according to the word of Hashem, (God) to the Courtyard of Confinement, and said to me, "Please buy for yourself my field that is in Anathoth, that is in the territory of Benjamin, for yours is the law of inheritance and yours is the law of redemption; buy it for yourself." And I knew that it was the word of God. So I bought the field that was in Anathoth from Hanamel, my cousin. I weighed out the money for him: seven shekels and ten silver pieces. <u>I wrote out the deed and sealed it,</u> and I designated witnesses; I then weighed out the money on a scale. I took the bill of sale, the one that was sealed according to the ordinance and the decrees, and the unsealed bill, and I gave the bill of sale to Baruch son of Neriah son of Mahseiah before the eyes of Hanamel, son of my uncle, and before the eyes of the witnesses who signed the bill of sale and before the eyes of all the Jews who were sitting in the Courtyard of Confinement."

"I instructed Baruch before their eyes, saying, "Thus said God, Master of Legions, God of Israel: take these documents this bill of sale, the sealed one and the unsealed document and place them in an <u>earthenware vessel, so that they will endure for many years. For thus said Hashem (God) Master of Legions, God of Israel: houses and fields</u> and vineyards will be bought in this land."

The <u>two documents</u> were drawn up to <u>attest</u> to the sale: first, the <u>sealed document transferred ownership;</u> second, the <u>unsealed document</u> attested that the sale was legal, uncontested, and binding.

The transfer and sale took place in the Courtyard of Confinement. The definition of confinement is: imprisoned, restricted or restrained and limited. The transgression of mankind brought man to a place of depravity, restriction, imprisonment and was most assuredly limited. He became a slave to his own soul. The light of God went out in his tabernacle. Righteousness no longer prevailed in the spirit of man. Innocents and holiness fell by the wayside as man was led by his soulish nature, not his spirit.

Symbolically Adam represented the spirit and Eve represented the soul. It was as if Adam, the spirit, never awoke from the slumber when Eve, the soul, was created. Man's spirit seemed to slumber; he was limited in his abilities without power, as a Son of God.

We see JESUS who entered the Courtyard of Confinement where we were imprisoned, paid the redemption price, and sealed the deed before designated witnesses. He gave a bill of sale and kept a bill of sale and the deed signed, sealed and delivered. <u>He placed the</u>

The Descent of the Sons of God (A Parable)

two documents in an earthen vessel, so they would endure for many years.

We, his sons, are always before his presence. We, his spirit, are in earthen vessels. As we stand before him, the bill of sale is open, eternally declaring, "this vessel was legally bought and paid for, nothing can reverse this sale, PAID FOR IN FULL!" The evidence of the sale is the deed, showing transfer of ownership, signed in his own blood.

Meditate on this for awhile… you were sealed, enclosed, fenced in by the Holy Spirit of promise, receiving a "holy spirit" never to be a slave again, no defilement, no misappropriation, no imprisonment from a perpetrator, or from your own soul; for the offense of the flesh was done away with at Calvary. No one can buy us, sell us, or steal us "we have two documents written upon our hearts, PAID FOR, NOT FOR SALE! SEALED BY THE HOLY SPIRIT!

So many times I hear people talk about the judgment day and how afraid they are that God will cast them into hell. How can God cast you into hell when the deed and the bills of sale are staring him in the face in your earthen vessel? Your spirit is your mark of SONSHIP! YOUR DEED IS THE MARK OF OWNERSHIP! He returned you to your "former estate;" now as Sons of God, build houses and plant fields and vineyards.

2nd Corinthians 3:2-3 reads, "Ye are our Epistle written in our hearts, known and read of all men: forasmuch as ye are manifestly declared to be the Epistle of Christ ministered by us, not written with ink, but with the spirit of the living God; not in tables of stone, but in fleshly tables of our heart."

Marye Nicholas

Revelation 20:12, "And I saw the dead small and great stand before God: and the books were opened: and another book was opened, which is the book of life: and the dead were judged out of those things which were written in the books, according to their works."

I have read these scriptures many times picturing the billions of books that were opened. I couldn't help but wonder where God kept all of those books. Could it be that he stored them on Pluto, or on several other planets? How many angels would it take to dispatch to carry the books? Since Father said he had us engrave in the palm of his hand why would he need a book; he said he knew his sheep and he was known of them, why would the creator that created the heavens and the earth have a memory problem and not remember names and faces, when he knew the numbers of the stars and calls them by their names. I pondered and pondered this and found the scripture in 2nd Corinthians and there was my answer! YOU are the Epistle of CHRIST written not with ink, but with the Spirit of THE LIVING GOD; not in tables of stone, but in fleshly tables of the heart.

Let me say it like this, it has been openly declared that you are demonstrating the truth, which is evident, apparent and obvious; that you are the Epistles of Christ written not with ink, but with the Spirit of the living God, not in tables of stones as Moses received from God in the mountain, but that which is being expressed through the flesh, the word of the Living God, the word of God in the flesh.

Children, we are the books that Jesus opens. We are his testimony his word in the flesh. When we stand before him, his word, his oracles, his precepts,

The Descent of the Sons of God (A Parable)

his principles, are opened before him, in us. Can God condemn his own word? WE ARE REWARDED!

THE BOOK OF LIFE WAS OPEN. WHAT IS LIFE? The Tree of life was in the midst of the garden. What is life? I come that you may have life more abundantly (John 10:10). He that believeth on me shall have everlasting life (John 6:40; 3:16). I am the bread of life (John 6:35). All of these scriptures speak of Jesus being life; he is that life, the Book of Life that we are talking about.

Could it be that we will be measured by the life of God in us? Ephesians 4:13 reads, "Till we all come in the unity of the faith, and of the knowledge of the Son of God, unto a perfect man, unto the measure of the stature of the fullness of Christ." The Father Son and Holy Spirit is the opened book of life. ALL his glory, righteousness and perfection will be gathered into one before his sons and daughters. We his books will be open and read before him, comparing spirit to spirit, the things we have learned and the measure of light we have walked in. Then, all other life will pale and become as nothing before him. LIFE WILL JUDGE DEATH, LIFE WILL SWALLOW UP DEATH. Thank God my name, identity and nature are written in him "the Book of Life." We are his little books, his Epistles sealed as Sons of God.

Many people are in fear of the Judgment Day. I don't look at that day in the future, I look at it in the here and now. I judge myself daily, moment by moment. One day I will step totally into my Father "the book" and begin reading him. I will see that a NEW DAY has dawned as I step into light brighter than the SUN. I will know instantly the whole creation plan from eternity to eternity. I will see the past, present and future and remember my origin when Father took me out of himself and held me in his hands cooing over me as he formed me first in the spirit, speaking to me in words of love as he prepared a body for me, that I would live in, to fulfill my destiny in the earth. I will remember how I looked into his eyes with all of the trust and love of a son going on a long journey, on a mission, to return again to his father of love; trusting his word that I would take my place in him once again.

In him will be perfection with joy unspeakable. Without death, we will be light and life; there will be no darkness at all. The word tells us that our God is a consuming fire, the fire will consume and destroy all evil. It also states, that hell will be cast into that fire. The hell you have suffered in your lifetime, the grave, plus past, present and future torment of hell. We will never think about DEATH, HELL OR THE GRAVE FOR IT WILL BE NO MORE! We will be the light and life of God, going throughout the earth, heavens and other worlds ministering to and healing the nations in the power and glory of the Sons of God!

The Descent of the Sons of God (A Parable)

PART TWO SCRIPTURE REFERENCES

Chapter 1 Hebrews 2:10 – St. John 17:6-17:17 – Acts 17:28 – Psalms 8 – Eph. 1:3-4-56 – Eph. 3:17-18-19 – Col. 2:9 – Romans 5:5 – Eph. 1:10 – Acts 17:28-29 – Hebrews 10:5 – St. John 10:34-35 – Psalms 82

Chapter 2 Hebrews 12:14 – Job 31-33 – Gen. 3 – Hebrews 7:10 – Acts 27:29-30 – 1 Peter 1:23 – Zech. 12:1 – Job 27:3 – Job 33:4-6

Chapter 3 Psalms 22:6 – Micah 7:16-17 – Matt. 12:34-23:33 – James 3:8-9-10

Chapter 4 Gen. 6:3 – St. John 10:2-7 – Rev. 4:1 – Luke 1:2 – Job 31:33 – Gen. 2 – Romans 5:10 – 2 Thes. 2:13 – Romans 3:23

Chapter 5 St. John 1:18 – Gen. 6:13 – Exodus 3 – Exodus 25 – Exodus 28 – St. John 10:12 – Ezk. 34

Chapter 6 Hebrews 10-39 – Matt. 10:28-16:28 – Prov. 16:17 – 1 Peter 1:9-4:19 – Eph. 5 – St. John 17:26 – Gen. 3:8-3:34 – Exodus 25 – Hebrews 6:9-10:20 – Luke 23:45 – Eph. 1:23 – Gen. 1:2 – Gen. 8 –

Marye Nicholas

              Phil. 3:14 – Exodus 33:18-22 – Luke 7:30-32 – 2 Sam. 24:16-17 – Isaiah 6:1 – Daniel 7 – Mark 1:13 – Luke 22:20-30 – Mark 10:38 – Isaiah 29:13 – Matt. 6-7 – James 1:8 – Matt. 14:23 – Mark 1:35 – Luke 9:29-22:32 – Romans 8:24 – Phil. 2:6 – Romans 8:14 – 1 John 3:1 – Mark 16:15-20 – Matt. 14:14-21-4:23-24-14:23-32 – Nehemiah 9:27 – Obidiah 1:21

Chapter 7   Matt. 16:19 – Eph. 1:17 – 1 Cor. 2 – Eph. 4:23 – Col. 3:10 – 1 Peter 1:23 – Luke 1:26 – St. John 6:63 – Gen. 3 – Luke 17:21

Chapter 8   2 Cor. 5:19 – Romans 5:10 – Cor. 1:20 – Psalms 34:1

Chapter 9   Col. 2:9 – 1 Cor. 6:19 – 2 Cor. 6:16 – 1 John 17 – 1 Cor. 4:7 – 2 Tim. 2:20 – St. John 2:17 – Romans 13:14 – Gal. 3:27

Chapter 10   Matt. 5:14 – Psalms 46:4 – 1 Peter 2:5 – Malachi 3:17 – Rev. 1:6 – Rev. 6:11

Chapter 11   St. John 3:27-31 – St. John 8:58 – St. John 14:7-9-10:30-38

Chapter 12   Luke 2:49 – St. John 8:16-29 – St. John 8:58 – Luke 6:13 – St. John 3:34 – Gal. 1:15-18 – Eph. 1 – 2 Peter 3:15-16 –

The Descent of the Sons of God (A Parable)

                Col. 1:13 – Gen. 37 – Eph. 1:10-13 – St. John 14:12 – St. John 14-17

Chapter 13   1 John 5:7 – Hebrews 9:24-28 – Eph. 1:13 – St. John 1:12 – St. John 10 – Isaiah 49:16 – Zech. 12:1 – Job 33:4 – Eph. 1 – Col. 2:12 – Daniel 7:10 – Hebrews 12:29 – St. John 5:1-5 – Revelations 22

Marye Nicholas

The Descent of the Sons of God (A Parable)

SUMMATION

Hebrew translation from the *Tanach, Torah Prophet Writings*, page, 1073 - Jeremiah (1:4) The word of Hashem (God) came to me saying, "Before I formed you in the belly I knew you, and before you left the womb I sanctified you; I established you as a prophet to the nations."

Before Jeremiah was born Father knew him, designated him for his destiny. He specifically took him out of himself for a special task or mission in the earth.

In Psalms ninety, verse one, there is a prayer by Moses, "Oh Lord, you have been an abode for us in all generations; before the mountains were born, and you had not yet fashioned the earth, and the inhabited land, and from the remote past to the most distant future, you are God."

In reading these scriptures we have to remember everything begins in the spirit realm first. We existed as a spirit millions of years before we entered flesh. Everything Father did and everywhere he went we were with him. He was filled with all power and we were filled with all power. When he created, rejoicing with explosions of laughter and praise over the works of his hands, we laughed and rejoiced with him. Everything was gathered together in him, he fulfilled all things. Nothing was separate from him; everything that existed and exists began first in him. He was and is the City of God, the temple and the people. We all came from him. He is the magnificent colors that shimmer and dance in his glorious light. The stones, the crystal sea, the angels and ministering spirits, sun, moon, stars and all universes, came out of him.

Before he created the earth and made the oceans, sea, springs, brooks and fountains; HE WAS THE FOUNTAINS OF THE DEEP. He would be the fountain of the deep to us, then, we who were created in his likeness would take on his likeness and become fountains of the deep to those about us. Although we would give forth from our fountain, we would be his fountains, fountains sealed unto him. He is the Tree of Life, the River of Life and the Garden. He has made us rivers of living water, fountains of gardens, cisterns and deep wells.

As a corporate body we are the fullness of him; he is the vine and we are the branches and his glory flows out from him, through our leaves, which is for the healing of the nations.

We are the Sons of his right hand, the BENJAMIN COMPANY. We have received the greatest portion. Father has waited for thousands of years to bring us into Goshen, the spirit realm of prosperity: spiritually and physically. He wants us to take the government upon our shoulders as full-grown Sons

The Descent of the Sons of God (A Parable)

ruling and reigning with him in power and glory in the heavenlies, in the earth and in the kingdom of light.

There are Sons in the earth that are recognizing their sonship, abandoning that which is earthly and focusing entirely on Father. Nothing takes priority in their lives, other than the word and intimacy with him; they know their destiny and true sonship. A choice has been made "it is all or nothing!" Soon a voice of a trumpet will sound and the Sons shall rise, and the confines of the flesh will fall away. Sons, as a mighty army will rise all over the earth to answer that call, marked with his name, nature and identity. In appearance they look as God himself, as they are the expression of his exact image.

God bless you my friends, may you prepare yourself now as SONS, to answer that call.

Marye Nicholas

About the Author

Marye Nicholas was raised in the traditional Holiness Denomination. Being a "Preacher's kid" she walked in the steps of her father, Reverend R. A. Norman who crossed over into the realm of the spirit in 1998. She has ministered as an Evangelist, Pastor, and teacher for many years and is the author of the book: *Back To The Garden Of Eden As Spiritual Partners*, published by Harrison House in Tulsa Oklahoma. Marye refers to it as "Her baby book" as she has grown so much since it was written.

In the last ten years Marye has recognized that the enemy is the mind, the soul. The soul lost its knowledge of its origin and identity when it transgressed. Therefore the soul became an entity of it's own, separating it's self from the Father. She believes the time of the soul was before the cross, and the time of the spirit is now. The soul is learning the things of the spirit through the word; lining up with its spirit and realizing it is a Son of God. When this revelation is comprehended to its fullest, man will fulfill his destiny in the earth and in eternity.

Printed in the United States
16628LVS00001B/44